KACI ROSE

Sunset

To the coffee that kept me going, and the kids that call me mommy.

Contents

Blurb

No matter what, I'm not opening up my heart again, even if he's great at warming my bed.

Jasper blew out-of-town, taking my heart with him. He swore he'd never come back. Last I heard, he was some famous chef in a big city.

Then, I'm at the farmer's market, and there he is in vivid color. So, I do what any sane person would do, I throw a kiwi at him and leave.

Then, a storm blows in, washing out the only bridge off this island, and now, we are stuck together.

To make matters worse. My chef quits, and the only option I have is to bring in Jasper, per his mother's suggestion.

Oh, and our mayor is trying to turn our small town into a major tourist spot. My best friend is in a fake relationship with a Hollywood movie star, and I just saw Jasper with his shirt off.

How did my life get here?

Get Free Books!

Do you like Cowboys? Military Men? Best friends brothers? What about sweet, sexy, and addicting books?

If you join Kaci Rose's Newsletter you get these books free!
Join Kaci Rose's newsletter and get your free books!
https://www.kacirose.com/KaciRoseBoB
Now on to the story!

Chapter 1

Brynn

No one ever wakes up and thinks, *'Today is the day I'm going to throw a kiwi at my ex boyfriend's head.* But yet, that's exactly what happened, and I don't regret a minute of it.

Farmer's Market days are my favorite. I like to do the shopping for my Inn myself, talking with everyone to see what's new in our small, little, beach town, and keep up on everyone. Recently, they added some craft booths, and there's always something fun and interesting going on.

I'm fighting between taking my time and rushing back to The Inn, because today is the day Kade Markson checks into my best friend, Lin's Sunrise Inn, which is next door to my Sunset Inn.

We run the Inn's together. She runs Sunrise, and I run Sunset, just like our parents did. Only our parents never had a mega movie star rent out the whole Inn for two weeks, even if it's off season.

So, after spending three days cleaning The Inn, and then checking on the suite he will be staying in, I welcomed the break today.

We can't tell anyone in town either, but this is the biggest thing to happen, since well sadly, since our parents died in the boating accident five years ago.

I shake my head, trying to listen to the people talking around me and making sure no sign of Kade's arrival has been leaked, but the talk is mostly of the storm coming up the coast, and how everyone is getting ready for it.

We had a really bad storm hit about five years ago, and ever since then, people take them a bit more seriously. Better to over prepare than to be unprepared again.

I stop at a booth and get some jam and pie filling that I know Lin will want to use in her baking. She makes breakfast for both Inns, and people rave about it constantly.

I'm getting ready to turn the corner, when the last voice I expected to hear, fills the air.

"My mom is on a kiwi kick, and she's going to love these." The masculine voice fills the air.

Jasper.

My ex-boyfriend who broke my heart. We had a plan, and when everything changed, he left for New York City anyway, leaving me here. Somehow, he blames Lin for not taking the entire burden herself and pushing me to go with him. I honestly don't know, because the fight we had didn't make much sense. Then, my parents died, and I just stopped trying.

He's been back to our small-town of Seaview a few times. We are on Hummingbird Island off the coast of North Carolina, and since there's only one bridge on and off the island, I guess it's too small for him. He never stays long, even after his father's funeral last year.

I try to back up and get away from him, but luck isn't on my side today. He turns his head and sees me, and his smile drops.

4

How is it possible this man looks even sexier today then he did the day we broke up? It's just not fair.

His square jaw has some stubble on it, and his dark, brown hair is a bit longer with some curl, and in the light, there are some red highlights in it. Of course, I'm in comfy clothes with my hair thrown up in a bun and no makeup on.

"Hello, Brynn." He says in a somewhat friendly tone.

This is a small-town and gossip is gold here, so of course, everyone around us freezes to watch what happens next. Then, they will run and tell anyone who wasn't here to witness what happened, and it will be the talk of the town all day.

Great.

"Jasper." I nod at him, and then pretend to look at the stand next to me.

"You're doing a shit job at ignoring me." He chuckles.

"I'm not ignoring you. I'm shopping."

"You're staring at mushrooms, and you're allergic to them." He says.

I finally focus on the stand in front of me, and he's right. Damn him.

I sigh and turn to him.

"What are you doing here in our tiny town? Shouldn't you be in New York?" I snap.

"My mom needed help this season with the restaurants, since my dad died, and she begged me to come back. So, I did." He shrugs.

"Oh, so that actually works? Someone needs you, and you come back. Funny, you had a different reaction, when I needed you."

"Come on, Brynn, not here." Jasper lowers his tone and looks around.

5

I don't care who sees us. I've been nice, gave smiles, and said all the right things, but something about him showing up today gets under my skin.

"You can't just leave the island to me? You can have the whole damn world, but you can't leave me alone to live my life in peace?" I grit out, taking a few steps towards him.

"Brynn, I grew up here, too. Right beside you, actually." He sighs and smartly takes a step back.

Something snaps inside of me. I swear, it's like I'm watching myself from outside of my body. This is the boy I gave my virginity to, the only boy I've ever slept with, the boy I had planned to marry, the one I loved, and the one who not only broke my heart, but stomped all over it, and he has the nerve to remind me we grew up together?

Before I realize what I'm doing, I grab a kiwi and glare at him.

"I know that, but it seems the second something flashy comes along, you're the one who forgot it. Damn you, Jasper!" I yell and launch the kiwi right at him. It hits his forehead, and everyone around us gasps.

He looks at me with irritation, as he rubs his forehead.

"Do you feel better now, Brynn? Get it out of your system?" He snaps.

"No!" I throw another kiwi at him, hitting his shoulder, and then turn and stomp off. I walked from The Inn wanting to enjoy the day. What the hell was I thinking? Now, I have to walk all the way back.

Oh. My. Gosh. Did I really throw kiwis at Jasper?

I totally did. I bite back a laugh and shake my head. My mom would laugh with me, while my dad would give me his stern face, saying I need to control my temper better. The temper I got from him, by the way.

God, I miss them.

I stare out at the water in the harbor, as I reach Main Street, trying to regain the peace I had this morning.

I love that our town's Main Street runs right along the water. It's been featured in many photos and paintings for this reason. While the water and I have a love hate relationship, I find standing downtown and taking it all in very comforting.

I turn to walk back towards The Inn, but the mayor comes out of a shop in front of me. I try to turn around to avoid him, because I know Lin has a meeting with him coming up, and he isn't too happy about it.

"Brynn, just the person I was looking for." Mayor Jones says.

Shit, twice in one day. I need better ninja skills.

Chapter 2

Jasper

I run my hand down my face. This is not how I expected the first time I ran into her to go. Fuck, she's more beautiful than the last time I saw her. She had no makeup on, and her hair was thrown up in a messy bun, but it's my favorite look on her. Always has been.

I rub my shoulder, where the second kiwi hit, and my face breaks into a smile almost all on its own. I taught her how to throw like that, when we were growing up, and she hasn't lost her touch. A sick part of me hopes it bruises, so I have her mark on me.

I turn to the boy managing the stand and pay for the kiwis, before going after Brynn. I promised my mom we wouldn't fight, and that I would talk with her and make things right.

My mom has always loved Brynn and seen her as a daughter, and I know after we broke up, she was there for both her and Lin, when their parents died. She has been working with Brynn the whole time I've been gone. It's how I was able to get my updates on her, which I craved, while I was gone.

Now that I have moved back, there's no way to avoid her.

My family has worked with Lin and Brynn's family with both Inns for years, and I know my mom is worried about that relationship. They send a lot of business our way. So, for my mom, I will fix this.

When my dad died, my mom begged me to come home. It took almost a year for me to convince myself it was time to head home, and to take over the family restaurants. It was always the plan, but I was too used to my life in New York City, and it was just far enough away from Brynn, and everything that reminded me of her and of us.

I turn the corner and find her stopped ahead of me, facing the harbor. From here, I can tell her eyes are closed, and I take a moment and soak her in. She's the most beautiful girl I've ever seen, and I've had many models pass through the kitchen in New York City. The restaurant owner dated them, like he was popping candy, a new one every weekend.

None of them compared to Brynn with her round face and dark, brown hair, which frames her face perfectly. She's grown it out, and I love the look on her. I remember the summer she tried bangs and hated it, refusing to ever do it again, but I thought she looked just as beautiful then, too.

She takes a deep breath and turns, putting her back to me and starts walking down Main Street. Here, in Hummingbird Island, our Main Street is the centerpiece. To my left, are shops, restaurants, including both my family's places, antique stores, and more. To my right, is the harbor, and the Atlantic Ocean just beyond that.

It's postcard perfect, and the quintessential hidden gem location for a summer vacation, which is why, the town is packed with families from Memorial Day to Labor Day every year, like clockwork.

The mayor steps out from a shop just in front of Brynn. She stops and tries to turn around and walk back towards me, but it's too late. Mayor Jones spots her.

"Brynn, just the person I was looking for." Mayor Jones says.

For some reason, I don't like the look on his face. It's not friendly. I vaguely remember my mom telling me about the mayor's plans to try and buy up the buildings on Main Street with a land developer, and then push out the Mom and Pop places and bring in large retail chains. That will mean putting us out of business, along with most families that live here year-round.

I guess, Lin and Brynn have been at the foreground fighting this, because their Inns are where most of the tourists stay, and they have almost more to lose than anyone else in town. The land developer would at least buy all of us on Main Street out, and we could start over, but their Inns would just die out.

I know they pitch the small-town life to their guests at both Inns, and that's what Seaview is known for. So, many of their guests come here just for that experience.

"Mayor. What can I do for you?" Brynn says, turning back towards him. I know that tone. It's the one that goes with her fake smile.

I don't think she saw me, so I walk up behind her, but give enough space, so as not to draw the mayor's attention.

"Miss Prescott has a meeting scheduled with me. Will *you* be joining her?" He asks, as his eyes run down her body, and I instantly know where his mind is.

I want to rip his eyes out for daring to leer at my girl. Wait, not my girl, but still mine to always protect. No matter what happens, she has always been mine to take care of, even if I've done a shit job at it recently.

10

"No, Mayor, I won't. But don't you worry, I was the one doing the research."

"I bet you were. You know I could help…" Knowing where his mind is going, I step in.

"I doubt she needs help from the likes of you." I snap, and both of their eyes turn towards me.

"Jasper?" Brynn asks, and I give her a nod. She has to know no matter what has happened between us, I won't allow another man to treat her like this.

"Mr. Adams, you can tell your mom I got her message. All twelve of them." He says.

"Well, you can tell her yourself by calling her back." I level him with a glare.

He stares back at me for a moment, before his cell phone rings.

"The wife always wants something," he grumbles.

"Maybe, you should get back to your *wife,* then," I tell him.

Without thinking, I put my hand on Brynn's lower back, just like I always used to do, as I guide her away from the mayor and further down Main Street.

"Where are you parked?" I ask her.

"I was handling that just fine, you know." She huffs.

"I know you were, but that doesn't mean you should have to deal with him either," I say, keeping my tone soft.

She shakes her head. "I don't need a ride. I walked."

"I'll walk you back to the Inn," I tell her.

"I'm a big girl, Jasper. Been taking care of myself all these years." She says.

The tightening of my chest has nothing to do with the guilt of leaving her to fend for herself. I'm just now beginning to understand what she went through, losing both her parents and Lin's parents in the boasting accident five years ago. I couldn't imagine both my mom and my dad dying at the same time. Losing my dad, has been hard enough.

"Humor me, okay?" I say, and she rolls her eyes at me and starts walking.

She still has the fire and spunk in her that drew me to her all those years ago. This is a dangerous situation.

Her Inn is on the water, so it's a straight shot on the sidewalk from Main Street. The sidewalk curves along the water with benches scattered along the way. Because of the view, it's a popular spot for people to take a stroll, or walk their dogs, and for joggers to run. The sidewalk dead ends at both Inns, which are at the end of the island. Our walk is over long, before I want it to be.

"Thank you for the escort, but I got it from here." She says with a trace of sarcasm in her voice.

"Listen, my mom wants to have lunch with you one day next week. I'm not going to be there, because she made me promise. So, pick a day, and I'll be banished to the restaurant."

She purses her lips and looks over my shoulder.

"Okay, I'll call her, because I like your mom. You, I can do without." She says.

"Goes both ways," I say and smile at her, before turning and making my way back into town.

Before heading home, I make a stop at the Farmer's Market and get the items my mom asked me to pick up. I know I have been away too long, because I have forgotten just how fast news travels in this town.

"Why the hell did Brynn throw not one, but two kiwis at you today in town?" My mom meets me on the porch. This tells me she has been waiting by the window for me to show up. She has always done this, when I'm in trouble.

"I don't know, Mom. Maybe, because I was breathing." I try to joke, as I head inside the cape cod style home.

"Well, I told you to fix things with that girl and not make it worse!" She hits me with the dishtowel in her hand.

"I'm trying, Mom, but all of this won't be fixed in one day. It will take time. She needed to throw the kiwis, so I just let her." I shrug, trying to ignore how ridiculous this all sounds.

"Did you tell her I want to have lunch with her?" She says her voice still irritated.

"Yes, she agreed and said she'd call you to set it up. I promised I wouldn't be there, so just let me know when, and I'll spend the day in the kitchen at one of the restaurants." I say.

"Good, good." Mom pauses, lost in thought. "She really threw two kiwis at you?" She asks, and when I turn to look at her, she's fighting a smile.

"Yep, just like I taught her, too. One to the forehead, and one to the shoulder." I rub my shoulder, like it hurts.

That's when my mom loses the battle and busts out laughing so hard, that she barely makes it to the dining room chair, before she collapses.

"That girl was always passionate. There's a fine line between love and hate, dear. You will do good to remember that." She says, when she finally calms down, and then stands to put the produce away.

I head to my room. I planned to stay in the space above one of the restaurants and turn it into a bachelor pad, but my mom guilted me into moving home and spending some time with her. She said the house is too big for just her. I think my mom knows I'll give her anything she wants right about now.

13

I walk into my childhood room, which thankfully, my mom had redecorated. It's no longer full of all the things that remind me of Brynn mixed in with photos of my dream culinary school and car posters. Now, it's a respectable nature green guest room that I find calming.

I sit down at the desk, intending on going over the books again from the restaurants, but I find myself on the Sunset Inn's social media page, hunting for any photo of Brynn that I can find.

Guests have tagged her in them, and she's shared some of her and Lin. My favorites are last season of her around the evening bonfire with guests. I continue scrolling, until I end up two years back, and I'm thankful to not find a single photo of her and another guy.

I don't know why, but that gives me some relief to think there hasn't been anyone, since me. I could ask around in town, but the last thing I need, is it getting back to her that I'm asking about her. Or worse yet, anyone in town getting any ideas about us and trying to stick their nose in it. No, thank you.

I'm not sure how I'm going to fix things between us. I did screw it up pretty badly, when I left the way I did it, and then, got upset that she didn't come with me. We barely spoke, when I came home for her parents' funeral. By then, she had completely shut down, and I can't blame her. At least, she let my mom and dad help her through it all. They kept me up-to-date, and I craved any little detail they would toss my way.

It shouldn't have taken me over five years to come back, and hopefully, I'm not too late to make this right. I will fix this, and not only, because my mom asked.

Chapter 3

Brynn

On the way to Jasper's mom's house, I start to wonder, if I can get out of this meeting. Lin doesn't need me, because Kade hasn't been as much of a diva, as we were expecting, but Mrs. Adams doesn't know that. Or I can say a pipe burst in a guest room. No, she'd send someone over to help fix it.

Each time I have an idea to get out of lunch, I know she has a way to take care of it. So, as I pull into her driveway, I've resigned myself to the lunch.

The town is a bit busier today, as everyone is still talking about the bridge that was washed out in the storm the other day. The bridge is our one way on and off the island. The town is split, as some are happy we are isolated from the mainland for a bit, and the other half are pissed they can't get off the island.

Supply wise we are fine, and we have a medical clinic if needed. Anything else major, the coast guard will airlift the person out. The county is working to get the bridge mess cleaned up and assess what can be reused.

This means Kade is trapped here awhile longer, too. Oh, joy.

Poor Lin. I sigh and glance up at the house in front of me.

I have so many memories at this house. Dinners with his family, spending time together, when his parents were working, study groups meeting here, and make out sessions in this driveway. They all assault me, as I stare at the classic white Cape Cod house with its black gabled roof, dormers, and shingle siding.

I step out of my car at the same time Mrs. Adams comes out of the front door.

"Come on, child. Lunch is waiting. We don't have all day for you to sit and stare at the old place." She says from her porch with a huge smile on her face.

Just like that, I'm eighteen again, as I run up the walkway to hug her. She's the closest thing I have to a mom right now, but with Jasper back in town, everything is changing.

"Let me get a look at you." She says, as she steps back and holds onto my upper arms.

"Too skinny as always, and still wearing those cut-off shorts that show off your legs. Men like a nice set of legs. Your boobs are a bit bigger too, or you've got a great push up bra."

"Mrs. Adams!" I gasp in fake shock.

"Oh no, dear. You call me Lisa."

"Okay, Lisa. It's my turn to take a look at you." I smile, as she stands up straight ready for inspection.

"Mmm, I think you have gotten an inch taller, or I shrunk! Still have those same curls in your hair, and you don't look a day over thirty-five. I don't know how you do it!"

"Oh, posh. Inside with you!" She laughs.

She does look good for her age. Her dark, blonde hair has gray in it now, and she has a few more laugh lines, but she has always been a few inches shorter than me with a stocky build. She says it's from all the southern cooking her husband made her eat. Without her morning walks, she'd be the size of a whale. Her words, not mine.

As I walk into the house, I can tell not much has changed. I take my shoes off in the foyer. Since we're a beach town, when you enter anyone's house, it's shoes off to keep the sand in the house to a minimum. It's just good manners.

The glass French doors open into the living room. There are more family pictures on the wall, and it has new furniture, but all in the same spots. She has redecorated, but all in all, it looks much the same.

I follow her into the kitchen that has been completely redone.

"Wow." I gasp, as I take it all in.

"Oh, yes. You haven't been here, since Samuel renovated it. It was right after Jasper left. The stove broke, and he demanded we have a chef's kitchen, since we had two chefs in the family, then. I agreed, and we ate at the restaurant for a month, while it was being done." She shakes her head.

I run my hands over the white granite tops, taking in the white cabinets.

"It has to be hard to keep clean." I think out loud.

"Not as bad as you think. Samuel insisted on some cabinets with dirt resistant something. You know he went on for an hour on how easy it would be to clean them. I finally agreed just to get him to change the subject!" She laughs, but there's a bit of sadness there, too.

"I'm so sorry," I say, and she just waves her hand at me and turns to pull the pitcher of sweet tea from the large stainless-steel fridge.

"It's God's plan, and it's brought my Jasper home to me, so

I'm thankful for that. But today, is not about bringing up old memories." She says, handing me a platter with her famous sandwiches and cookies on it, as I follow her to the already set dining area.

They have a formal dining room, but they always eat in this dining nook. It has a u-shaped bench seat surrounded by windows on three sides, and a few chairs on the fourth side. It's both comfy and welcoming.

"Now, dear, you know there are no secrets in this town." She gives me her mom look.

I sigh, "I will apologize to Jasper about the kiwis." I say, as I take a sandwich and some cookies onto my plate.

She pours me some sweet tea, and then sets the pitcher down.

"You will do no such thing. That boy deserved it!" She says to my shock.

I can't help it, as I burst out laughing.

"Now, tell me what's new with you and Lin?" She says.

We spend a few minutes going on about changes at The Inn. I'm careful not to mention Kade staying there, or anything outlined in the non-disclosure I had to sign.

"Now, I heard that Lin gave a bunch of her employees two weeks paid vacation spur of the moment. Is everything okay?" She asks.

Shoot, I don't want to lie to her, but I'm under a non-disclosure and don't have a choice.

"Oh, yes. She decided to do some last-minute renovations, before the season starts, and since her employees hadn't taken time off this year, she thought it was good timing." I recite the spiel Lin and I worked on for when people in town started asking questions.

Lisa seems to buy it, as we finish up our first sandwich and each take a second one.

"You know, Jasper is trying to come to terms with his dad's death. He hates he wasn't here." Lisa says.

"He couldn't have known he'd have a heart attack like that," I tell her.

"That's what I've been telling him. He dropped everything to come home as soon as he heard, but by the time he got here, his dad was gone." Lisa's eyes get a bit misty.

"You know, a few weeks after he moved home, he got drunk one night after dinner, and we were talking, and he went on and on about how he now understands how you felt, and how much he hates himself for the way he treated you. He said he should have moved home right away and all sorts of other stuff."

I don't know what to say, so I just shake my head and play with the cookies on my plate.

"He never told me the details behind you two breaking up, you know. I can guess, but he never talked about it." She says, looking at me. I know this is her gentle nudge to get the details, and I guess, she does deserve them.

"Ahhh, there isn't some big mystery. You know my dad got sick with the flu and ended up in the hospital right when Jasper and I had plans to move away. I said I didn't want to leave, while my dad was sick and asked him to put off moving for a week or two. He said he couldn't, because of the job he had lined up. I told him to go, and I'd meet him there as soon as my dad was better, and he agreed. We talked every night, and sometimes even during the day." I pause, thinking of those times.

"Then, I remember my dad got home, but he still wasn't able

to run The Inn, and I was helping my mom out, so I decided to stay a bit longer. Lin agreed that I should stay and help out. That night I told Jasper, and we fought. He blamed Lin for getting it in my head that I needed to be here, when I didn't. I was so mad that he wanted me to leave my dad, while he still wasn't back on his feet, and Jasper said I should think about what was more important. So, I hung up on him, because there was no question that my dad was more important."

"I raised him better than that," she shakes her head.

"It was hard handling the long distance. I didn't want to be away from him any more than he wanted to be away from me, and I think he just pinned the anger on Lin, so he didn't pin it on me. Anyway, he called a week later, asking when I was moving out. I said I wasn't, because the answer to his last question was that my family will always be more important. Then, we hung up. I guess, I expected the big romantic gesture you see in the movies, but one week turned to two, and then it turned into a month. Then, my parents died, and I still held out that he'd come home, after the funeral, but I never heard from him."

"I think he was waiting on you to show up on his doorstep. He never stopped asking about you. Especially, after your parents died, and we were helping you girls get everything organized. You know, he was at the funeral, too."

"Yeah, we talked for a moment. I told him there was no way I could move now, and that I was going to run The Inn. That was when I knew it was the end, because he said he wasn't ready to move home. I still hoped, though." I admit.

"You haven't dated since then though, have you?" She asks.

"I have been out on dates, but they all sucked, or we didn't have any sparks. So, no, nothing more than one or two dates."

I tell her.

"Jasper hasn't dated either. Nothing he's told me about, or anything on his social media. A mother always stalks her child's social media." She winks at me, letting me know she stalks mine, too. Though, mine is The Inn's and not a personal one.

We finish eating, and she sits back in her chair.

"There's something else you aren't telling me. I can see it in your eyes." She narrows her eyes at me.

"Fine! My chef at The Inn quit. He got selected to go on some reality TV show out in Hollywood and just left. I begged him to stay on, until the bridge reopened, so I could get someone else out here, but he refused, saying he plans to watch all the old episodes, so he can strategize. Lin says we should watch the show, because she thinks he will fail epically. I also told him don't come to me for a reference. He's so sure he's going to win. If he doesn't, there will be four years he will have to leave off his resume with me, because I'll tell them exactly how he left."

"Serves him right!" She says.

"You don't happen to know any unemployed chefs on the island right now, do you?" I sigh. "Between Lin, me, and my kitchen staff, we can do a limited menu, but it won't be great."

"I actually do know someone. I will call as soon as we are done and see if they are willing to help. In fact, I know I can twist their arm!"

I should have known by the gleam in her eyes that this would be trouble.

When will I ever learn?

Chapter 4

Jasper

I walk into the house, and my mom is sitting at the kitchen counter. She does this, when she's waiting on me, and always has, since I was a kid. This time she's making a list, probably menu planning meals for anyone who needs them.

"How was your lunch?" I ask, wanting to know how things went with Brynn, but not wanting to seem too eager to know the details.

"It was good. We were talking about old times. We talked about you, of course, and what's new at The Inn. Then, she told me the strangest thing." She says with a twinkle in her eyes, which I know means trouble.

"What's that?" I ask, pulling a bottle of water from the pantry. After working in a hot kitchen, I prefer to drink room temperature water. My dad was the same way.

"I guess, her chef at The Inn quit, after being there for four years. He got picked for one of those reality TV shows, and then left her high and dry, since she can't get anyone onto the island right now."

Danger Will Robinson sirens start going off in my head, and I can't get a word in, before she continues.

"So, I got to thinking that the new sous chef you hired is good and should be given a chance in the kitchen." Mom continues.

"He is good. What are you getting at?"

If she's suggesting I send him over to Brynn's to help out, I think I could do that with the stipulation he's to come back to me, as soon as she gets a new chef. I don't want to lose him, because I plan to make him the main guy in the kitchen, when I'm not there.

"I know your plans are to put him in charge, when you aren't there, so do it, and then you go help Brynn."

"Wait, what?" I say, processing her words.

"You promised to work things out with her, and this is the perfect chance. She's in a bind, and you can help her out. It's the best way to apologize for being a jerk all those years ago."

"Whose side are you on?" I mumble.

"We both know you deserve more than the two kiwis she tossed at your head. Do this for me, if you won't do this for yourself." She starts laying on the guilt nice and thick.

"I need to think about this," I say, and without another word, I turn and head out of the back door, taking the footpath that leads to the beach.

I walk aimlessly, trying to put all this together. But the more I think of sending another guy into Brynn's kitchen to help out, the more I hate the idea.

Can I handle all of that time in close proximity with her? It will be for at least two to three weeks. I know the county and state are rushing the bridge with it being the only way on and off the Island, but there's the possibility it could be more than that.

The dream we had as kids was to get out and work on the

23

mainland for a few years. When Brynn was ready to take over The Inn, we'd move back, and I'd run the kitchen, while she ran The Inn. We'd work together just like her parents did. Then, when my parents retired, I'd manage the two restaurants, and we'd run it all together.

Lin had the same plan with her then boyfriend, Travis. The four of us were inseparable, until Brynn's dad got sick. Then, her parents died, and Travis broke up with Lin at her parents' funeral. I gave him two black eyes the next day, and that was the end of our friendship. He's back in town too, and I hope he doesn't try and start problems for Lin, because I'm happy to give him a repeat performance.

I end up by the graveyard and head in to go see my dad. It's always hard to see his name on the stone. The empty plot next to him will be my mom's, and I know that day will kill me.

"Hey, Dad," I say, sitting down next to him on the cool grass.

"I know you can see what's going on, and I know you're watching over Mom. Heck, it was probably you who put the idea in her head about me working at The Sunset. I know how much you loved Brynn, and how upset you were, when we broke up. I promised Mom that I would make things right with her, but I don't think working side-by-side with her is a good idea."

I pause, trying to think of the reasons why.

"Well, for one, a kitchen has knives, and they are worse than getting hit with kiwis. I hate to see what she throws at me next, and we both I know deserve whatever it is."

That's the only argument I have, and it's a weak one. "I love you, Pops," I say, standing up, and I start walking again with no place in mind. I don't pay attention, as I think about how long I waited for her to show up on my doorstep, saying she missed me.

Even after her parents died, I waited, even though I knew in my heart, it wouldn't happen. I tried dating in New York City, but city girls just aren't my thing. The endless string of models my boss dated didn't appeal to me. They were so fake, where Brynn is real, and what you see is what you get.

None of the girls in New York City even came close to Brynn, so I stopped dating and tried to focus on work. I planned to stay in the city for two more years, before coming home to learn from my dad. I'd take over and let him retire early and enjoy time with my mom. I figured once I was back in the South, it would be easy to find a good girl to settle down with.

Then, my dad died, and seeing Brynn at the funeral, broke me. I finally understood all she went through. I also realized why none of the girls I dated were good enough. Because standing there with tears running down her face, in that black dress, and the same one she wore to her parents' funeral, I knew I was still in love with Brynn.

It's why I resisted for a year about coming home, when my mom asked. I needed to be prepared to run into her, or even to see Brynn dating someone else. I know I blew my chance with her and had to prepare myself for that reality, before I came home.

By the time I look up, I realize The Sunset Inn is right in front of me. Of course, my subconscious brings me here. I sit down on a nearby bench and just stare at the building that was a second home to me growing up.

I had the run of the place, since I was a kid, and even more so, when Brynn and I started dating. Summers by the pool and on the beach were plentiful. Brynn has done a great job keeping The Inn up, since her parents died. I heard her and

Lin were running them together still, and it's just like their parents had.

I'm so damn proud of her. Her dream was to always run this Inn, and while she was thrown into it much sooner than expected, she has hit the ground running and is now living her dream.

I can help her with this dream, right? Just for a few weeks, I can have a taste of that dream we always had together. Maybe, that brief time would be enough to hold me over.

I get up and start making my way home. Thankfully, I don't run into anyone who wants to stop and talk. Most just nod and continue on their way.

I turn down my street, as memories of many days just like this of walking home, after making sure Brynn got in okay, flash into my mind.

On the north end of our island, there's a state park with a natural arch rock and protected beach. There are many undeveloped lots owned by locals, so there's a few walking or hiking trails. The south tip of the island is where The Sunrise and Sunset Inns are, while Main Street is in the middle on the east side of the island. The rest of the island is mostly residential streets.

In school, if you were in any sports, it was nothing during Saturday practice to 'run the island.' You can walk from the north side to the south side in about thirty minutes, and east to west in around twenty minutes. So, it's good exercise to run around the island. If we were in trouble, we had to do it on the sand.

So, growing up as kids, we learned quickly that we could go anywhere just by walking. My parents always told me to make sure Brynn got home okay, even if it made me late for curfew.

They eventually made my curfew thrifty minutes after hers.

Lots of good memories. Mom would always be waiting for me on the front porch. Sometimes, she'd have fallen asleep and always pretend she hadn't, when I woke her up.

I step into the house, and the smell of my mom's spaghetti fills the air. My dad and I may be the chefs, but my mom knows how to cook too, and no one makes better spaghetti than her. We aren't even allowed to use her recipe at the restaurants, because she made us swear to it.

"Hey, Mom," I call out.

"Hey, baby. Good timing. Dinner is almost done." She says.

I check the clock, and I hadn't realized I'd been gone that long.

"I had some things to do. Went and visited Dad." I tell her. She just nods, as I help set the table.

"I'll do it just until she can hire someone, but this will be the extent of your matchmaking, you hear me?" I say in as stern of a voice as I dare to my mother.

"If you say so, dear. I'm just glad you decided to do the right thing. Even without your history, I'd have suggested the same thing, because we were good friends with her parents, and I made them a promise to look after her." She says.

"What?" I ask.

"One day, when the girls were about ten, Brynn's grandma was put into a nursing home. Lin and Brynn's parents both came to me and asked if anything were to happen to the other, would your father and I be willing to take in Brynn and Lin? We agreed, and I promised, if I outlived them, to look after the girls. They made me the same promise about you."

"How did I not know this?" I ask.

"Oh, you were only eleven yourself, and it's not something

parents share with their kids."

"After dinner, I'm going to go to the restaurants and get everything set up, so I can go to The Sunset for lunch tomorrow," I tell my mom.

"Sounds good, baby. I'm going to go play bingo at church tonight."

"Say a prayer for me, while you're there. I'm going to need it." I tell her.

Chapter 5

Brynn

I had no idea how much work went into lunchtime around here. I suggested sandwiches, trying to keep the menu easy. Well, two ladies can't have bread, we have a vegetarian, and someone who only eats Keto. I had to look that one up.

There's a couple who don't like sandwiches but wants burgers. Isn't that just a hot sandwich? Then, there are sides, fries, and of course, we have to go and make our own chips. Whose idea was that?

After burning the second batch of fries, I toss them into the trash with a screech. When someone chuckles from the doorway, I look up ready to tear into them, only to find Jasper, leaning against the door frame.

"What the fuck are you doing here?" I ask him, as one of the kitchen guys takes the fry basket from me.

"Mom told me about your chef. I'm here to help, until you hire someone else. No strings attached." He says.

"Oh, there are always strings. I should have known your mom would do this, when I asked if she knew anyone." I turn around and find Ken, my head waiter, watching us.

Ken knows all and sees all. His boyfriend works at the front desk, so he has all the gossip.

"That's so sweet, and we need the help. We'll be losing money on Brynn's fries alone. Who let her in the kitchen?" He grabs his plates and heads back out to the dining room.

If he wasn't great at his job and been with me for the last six years, I'd fire him. But he'd just show up for work the next day and laugh. I know, I've tried it.

"Listen, you need help. We have things covered on our end, so let me help you," he says.

"You need a chef, Brynn. Just let him help," Ken says, walking back in.

I glare at Jasper and grab Ken's hand, pulling him back into the chef's office and closing the door behind me. He may be taller than me, but he's as skinny as me, and I'm easily able to drag him around.

"What are you doing? The last person we need in the kitchen is him!" I hiss.

"But he's the best on The Island, and you know it. You need help. No one in there is prepared to take over a kitchen. George wouldn't train them, because he liked keeping them down and unprepared. Good riddance to him, if you ask me. So, let Jasper train them and get the kitchen running. He knows what he's doing."

Ken says, while using the mirror on the back of the door to check his hair. Not a strand of his jet-black hair is out of place.

"Anyone but him." I shake my head.

Ken pulls me into a hug. This might not be normal boss employee behavior, but Ken is also a friend outside of work, and we are a small-town, so boundaries cross a lot.

"Listen, I know you two have a history, and it won't be easy. But with him in the kitchen, you don't have to be. You can focus on helping Lin with Mr. Blue and leave Mr. Kiwi to me."

I burst out laughing. Lin and I named the guys the other night. Mr. Blue is Kade, because the fancy car he drove in with is blue. Mr. Kiwi is Jasper, because he took those kiwis so well.

"Don't do this for you. Do this for your parents. You know they liked Jasper, despite everything he's done, so let him help you. I'm sure he has a need to make things up to them, too. He might need this more than you think." Ken says.

I hug him tighter, before I pull away. Why does he always have to make sense?

"Fine. Now, what's the gossip for today?" I ask, needing a distraction, before I go back up there.

"The couple in room four called to complain that the couple in room three were having sex too loud last night. Turns out, the wife wasn't there, and the husband had picked up some girl no one knows. I think it was Jessica, but we can't prove it, yet."

Lin and I went to school with Jessica, and she was the typical mean girl. But in small-towns, karma works its magic. She was pregnant at graduation and 'went to visit her grandma' that summer, which was code for having the baby and adopting it out, before getting back in shape and coming home. She hasn't changed one bit.

"Also, the couple in The Sunset Suite hasn't been seen for two days. They just order room service. Housekeeping has disinfecting spray on hand, when they check out. Though, everyone has extended, because of the bridge."

Oh yes, we had to discount our rates, because where were

these people going to go?

"So far, no complaints, but if it goes on another week, I'm going to have to offer some even deeper discounts and some comped rooms. Okay, well, I'm getting back out there. Thanks." I say.

I step back into the kitchen, and Jasper has already taken over and is plating a hamburger. The guys in the kitchen are all smiling and laughing. Great. In ten minutes, he's already won them over. I glare at them.

"Traitors. All of you." Then, I stomp out and down to my office. I slam the door, even though there's no one around to hear it and try to get some work done.

Emails and social media take my mind off the man in my kitchen for only a short time, before it's all I can think about again.

I know the kitchen is getting ready for their dinner rush right now, so I head in and find Jasper in the kitchen office.

"These books are a mess. Did you ever look at them, or did you trust him blindly?" Jasper says without even looking up.

"He imported everything to the computer, which I monitor. I don't know what he keeps written down, and I never cared how he did his system. It's the stuff that's entered into the computer that we monitor. I watched the inventory, and also the money in and money out that way." I tell him.

"Log me in?" He asks, nodding towards the computer. When I hesitate, he finally looks over at me.

"Brynn, I'm just trying to help. I want to make sure this guy wasn't screwing you over, because I can't make sense of all this. I also need to see what our inventory is, and then make some menus to use up what we have," he says in a soft tone.

I know he's right, so I get him logged in, and he starts poking around.

All I can do is watch him, as he clicks around the screen and takes in the data. I won't admit to him that I'm glad to have another set of eyes on the books, especially, after how George left.

"Okay, your food waste is a bit high. I think we should run some reports, and then cut the lowest selling items from the menu." He says.

"Which items would that be?" I ask him, as I step into the office, leaning on the side of the desk, and then cross my arms and watch him.

"The tuna, the lasagna, and the supreme pizza. I'd also cut the catfish from the kid's menu." He says, and finally, his eyes look up at me.

Damn him. Because moments like this, are the ones we were supposed to have in our future. Running The Inn together, exactly like this.

"Fine, make it happen. Redo the menu, and I can print them in my office, until the mail opens back up," I say and turn to leave.

Being so close to him, is fogging my brain and not letting me think clearly.

"Brynn…" He says, stopping me in my tracks.

"What?" I ask over my shoulder.

"Is this how it's always going to be?" He asks.

"Well, considering it's five years later, and I've yet to hear an apology out of your mouth, I'd say yes, exactly like this." I leave the office, as my heart starts to race.

I march into the kitchen, grabbing my dinner plate, and then heading to my room. I lock the door, as I plan on being in for the night. I turn on some reality TV show and try to get lost in someone else's problems for a change. I finish my burger, which I have to admit, is one of the best I've ever eaten, and that irritates me even more.

I turn off the TV, grab my tablet, and decide to take a nice hot bubble bath and read, until my skin is all pruny. I get a few chapters in, when someone starts pounding on my door.

I don't move. If it's Lin, she has a key, and if it's not, then I have no intentions of getting out of this water and opening the door.

"I know you're in there, Brynn," Jasper yells. I check the time, and sure enough, the kitchen should be closed by now.

"Fine, don't answer, but we need to talk at some point. I'm sorry about what happened. I was young, stupid, and just didn't understand it all. You were always more mature than me, you know that, and how you put up with me all those years, I will never know, but I'm grateful you did. When you're ready to talk, I'll be right here, but I'm just warning you, we will talk." He says.

"Not on your life," I whisper, knowing he can't hear me.

"I'm not going anywhere, and you're just going to make this harder on you and your employees the longer you fight this." He tries again.

I still don't answer, waiting to see what he says next.

"Fine, Brynn, but this isn't over." He growls.

I know that growl, and my body knows that growl, so I gasp. He would growl like that in bed. My body betrays me, as my nipples stiffen, and my core starts to throb.

No, I refuse to give in, as I force myself to think about walking into the supply closet and finding that eighty-year-old couple, going at it two summers ago. All the saggy skin and wrinkles is exactly the picture that stops my body in its tracks.

I lean my head back on the edge of the tub. He's right. I know we need to talk, but I don't know what to say. I want to forgive him, and I thought I had a long time ago. But seeing him here in person, I'm not so sure I actually did. Maybe, I convinced myself I did just to make me feel better. I also know that a small part of me knows, if I forgive him, then that leads to me opening up to him, and I can't trust him with my heart again.

I finally get out of the tub and go to bed. This is going to be a long few weeks. I'm going to put out an ad for a new chef tomorrow. I can do interviews over video and have someone lined up the moment the bridge opens.

That's the only way I'm going to survive this.

Chapter 6

Jasper

I've been working here at The Sunset in the kitchen for a week now, and I've got a good routine going with the guys. Brynn has a great staff, but the problem is that the last chef wasn't willing to teach them. They're hungry to learn, and they learn fast.

My goal has been to train them on everything, so if God forbid something like this happens again, she isn't left in the lurch. I've also been revamping her menu a bit and lowering her food costs. She has resorted to communicating with me via The Sunset's messaging system and by email.

That's fine, as she obviously needs some time. The more I'm here, the more I know I was an idiot, and this is where I should have been all along. I got blinded by the big city lights and fancy titles.

We wrap up dinner service, and I decide to head out to the back porch and take in the waves, before I dig into the inventory. We have been readjusting the menu each night based on what we have, and what needs to be used. Brynn was on the right track, when she suggested a limited menu, and so far, there have been no complaints, as long as we have gluten-free, vegetarian, and Keto options for those few guests.

The night is quiet, and everything almost seems still, except for the crashing of the waves. This back porch was my favorite place at night growing up. My parents would be in talking to Brynn's, and we would sit out here and play cards and games. Later, we would make out in the corner.

I'm surprised to find Brynn out here on the couch with a glass of wine in her hand. She looks at me, but she doesn't say anything. Since she isn't telling me to leave, I sit in the chair next to her, and take in a deep breath of fresh, salty, sea air.

"Thank you for helping this week in the kitchen." She says.

"You're welcome. I think I got all the bookwork and paperwork in order. I have a sample menu ready for when the bridge is back open. It will lower your food costs, while allowing you to charge more. I don't think George was doing much of anything at the end there." I tell her.

"No, apparently, he was too busy filming his audition for the reality TV show. I hope he's cut first round. I told him not to bother to call for a reference. No way will I give him a good one, and now, he'll have four missing years on his resume to explain." She huffs.

"What if he wins? You could try to capitalize on it." I tell her.

Then, she does the last thing I expect. She busts out laughing.

"He's not a team player, his food was subpar at best, and he never came up with new recipes. I recently found out Ken was the one to push him to put new things on the menu. The devil you know, right?" She shakes her head.

I try not to think about how she wouldn't be in this mess at all, if I had come back to help her, when she needed it, or if we had changed our plans and just pushed ahead sooner.

"So, tell me, why are you doing this? And don't give me the spill about, oh my mom made me crap." She says.

"Mom's idea was to send over our sous chef and test him out on running a kitchen, but then somehow, she twisted it to me coming over. I did some thinking and decided I'd rather it be me here than someone else. I've made many mistakes, but I plan to start making them right." I tell her honestly.

We sit in silence for a few minutes, and I think back to when I brought food to her room the other day, and Kade was in her room. Apparently, he's dating Lin, and they aren't hiding it, but it doesn't explain why he was in Brynn's room that night. So, I decide to go for broke.

"So, Kade?" I start.

"What about him?"

"I thought he was dating Lin," I say.

"He is." She says, and bites back a smile. She knows what I want to know, but she's going to make me work for it. *Typical Brynn.*

"Why was he in your room?" I ask, trying to keep as calm as possible.

"Lin was in the bathroom, when you came to the door. She timed it perfectly. Watch out for her, because I think she's playing matchmaker."

"Like you weren't doing the same for her and Kade," I tell her. "You know, you should be careful. He has a reputation for a reason. I wouldn't be so quick to push him on your best friend." I say.

I looked up everything on Kade Markson. He's labeled Hollywood's Playboy, and there's picture after picture with him and a different girl each night on his arm.

"Really? Oh, right, you weren't here, when the press hounded Lin and me for months. You didn't see the stories they made up, and the shit they printed. They hid out in trees, trying to get a photo at just the right angle to make up whatever story they wanted. Just because it's printed doesn't make it true." She snaps.

"I'm just trying to watch out for you!"

"Oh, yeah. How? By sabotaging every interview I've tried to set up. Is that looking out for me? The bridge is going to open, and I'm still not going to have a chef!" She yells.

I did look over every application she was setting up a video interview with, and I knew a few of them, and they weren't right for the job. One I didn't want around Brynn at all. Two others thought they were so high and mighty their egos wouldn't fit through the door, when I talked to them. Another had never worked at a place with fresh seafood.

"You need someone who doesn't have an inflated ego, who has worked with fresh seafood, and who doesn't mind a small-town. Preferably, a family man or woman, because this isn't a place for a playboy or someone single. You don't want someone too new, because then this will just be a stopping point on the way to New York City, Vegas, or Hollywood. You also have to be careful about Kade, and that they aren't trying to get to him and his contacts."

"So, basically you. Oh, wait, your inflated ego rules you out." She rolls her eyes.

I haven't had anyone roll their eyes at me in years. It makes me want to take her over my knee and give her a lesson on what happens, when she gets bratty with me. Brynn is too stubborn for that, though.

She chugs down the rest of her wine in two large gulps, and

then stands up.

"Why can't you just let me be and let me hire who I'm going to hire?" She yells.

"Why so you can be in the same position next season?" I bite back.

I stand up and turn to leave. I'm almost to the door, when I hear her growl, and a potted plant hits the wall inches from my head.

That's the moment Lin rounds the corner. Her eyes are wide, as she stares at the plant.

"She's all yours." I snort, shaking my head.

* * *

Brynn

"Chill out, our insurance doesn't cover PMS," Lin says with a hint of a smile on her face.

I flip her off and pour another glass of wine, as Lin sits down next to me. Her blonde hair almost glows in the moonlight, and there's happiness in her eyes that hasn't been there, since our parents died.

"So, how are things going with Kade?" I ask her.

"Oh, no. You first. You don't get to throw a potted plant at someone and not talk about it." She says.

"I had six video interviews lined up. Perfectly good chefs, and he sabotaged every one of them. I think the kitchen staff likes him better than they like me. And he's lowered our food cost, he's redoing the menu, and his burgers are better." I pout.

In my head, I know these are all small things. Well, except for him sabotaging my interviews, but they all add up over the course of a week and really start to get under my skin. It's why I was out here to begin with, to get away from him and enjoy the calm of the beach at night. Of course, he ruined that, though.

"Do you remember the chef your dad hired, before George?" She says.

I think back. His name was Andrew, and the first change I made was firing him.

"Yeah, he was friendly with everyone, but his food sucked."

"He was a little too friendly with some of the female staff," Lin says. "But the point is, your dad liked him as a person, but his cooking left something to be desired. Then, you got George. His cooking was good, but his people skills were lacking. Now, you have the best of both worlds, and you can't wait to get rid of him."

"He's not staying. He's just on loan. If it was anyone but Jasper, I'd fight for them to stay. But not Jasper, besides, he has his own restaurants to run." I tell her.

"Do you remember the summer we found my mom's romance book collection? We read through so many books that summer, and never left my room." She smiles.

"I noticed my mom had a lot of enemies to lovers' books, and I just didn't understand it. So, one day after she caught us reading them, I asked her about them. She said there's a fine line between love and hate, and many times, the person who is angry at the other is using that anger, as a shield to protect themselves from being hurt."

"You're talking about me, aren't you?"

She just smiles.

"Okay, your turn. How is your fake dating going?" I ask in an attempt to change the subject.

When Kade's publicist pushed for him to fix his image with a fake relationship, one thing led to another, and with some pushing from me, Lin was the lucky girl. It's perfect with the bridge still out, and the press can't hound us.

The problem is I see Lin falling, and I'd be worried, if I didn't see the way Kade looks at her. It's the way Jasper used to look at me. The bonus is her ex is back in town, and he's a big fan of Kade's movies, and it's driving him insane that they're together.

"It's going good. He's a lot nicer than I thought he'd be. I took him up to the arch, and we... um... well, we... kissed." She stutters.

"Well, yeah, kissing is what seals the relationship with the people in town," I tell her.

"No, there was no one around." She says, and even with the limited light, I can see the red stain on her cheeks.

Ahhh, so they kissed for themselves, and not for the sake of a fake relationship. So, it is getting a bit more serious.

"Well, enjoy it, but keep your heart out of it," I tell her, even though I know it's useless.

"I could tell you the same thing." She smiles.

We sit in the quiet and stare out at the water. What a week it's been.

Chapter 7

Brynn

What on Earth am I doing? I haven't been on a date in years. I had a few bad first dates, after Jasper and I broke up, and I gave up on dating, and threw myself into working at The Inn.

Now that the bridge is back open, Kade went home to Hollywood. He got some major movie roles and left a note saying goodbye. I will say, I'm a bit pissed off. He and Lin had transitioned from a fake relationship to a real relationship, and it was obvious to me and them how much they liked each other.

I know they had sex, because Lin told me. Not only did they have sex, but it was also amazing sex. *Lucky bitch.* But now that he's gone, it's like she needs a distraction, so she set me up on a date. I'd have refused, if she wasn't so damn heartbroken.

His name is Daniel, and he's Joe and Martha's son. They own the pharmacy downtown, and Daniel is in school to be a pharmacist, like his dad and take over the family business.

That's how it happens here in Seaview; the next generation takes over a successful family business. Lin and I took over The Inns, Jasper his dad's restaurants, Daniel the Pharmacy, and Ned the newspaper from his dad. While Nate became a cop, like his father, and he will probably run for sheriff, when his dad retires.

It's the cycle of small-towns with successful businesses. Daniel doesn't seem like a bad guy. He's a local, so that makes things easy, and he'll have a successful job, once out of school, but that's the problem. He's still has a year left in school. Normally, that would mean he's a year older than me. But apparently, he's super smart and did summer courses and is graduating early.

Both the town and my best friend are so desperate for me to date, they are now pairing me with guys younger than me by two years. If this keeps up, the boys are going to graduate high school, and the town will start throwing them my way.

Maybe, Lin had the right idea of a fake relationship to get people off my back.

I take a deep breath and step out of the bathroom to show my outfit to Lin, who is sitting on my bed. When she looks up, she jumps up and rushes over to me.

"Oh, Brynn, you look beautiful! It's just the perfect amount of casual and dressy." She says.

I'm in darn near skintight jeans paired with a dark purple silk top and heels. I kept my hair down, but I put some beach waves in it. Though, I didn't want to try too hard, I did want him to know I put some effort into our date.

Just then, my phone in my room rings. The phone is attached to The Inn, so I know it's one of my staff, and I pray there's nothing wrong, because I could use a night away.

"Hello?" I answer.

"Your date is here to pick you up," Rich says, and I can hear the smirk in his voice.

Rich is my front desk manager and Ken's boyfriend, so I know as soon as I leave this will be the talk of the night. Rich is also on my side and doesn't believe in pushing people to date, so he's been my go-to, when I want to complain about this.

"Thank you." I hang up and turn to Lin.

Her eyes are still sad, no matter how much of a smile she tries to force for my sake.

"How about you hang out here, and after my date, I will raid the kitchen for dessert and some wine, and I'll tell you every detail, as we eat ourselves into a sugar coma?" I ask.

Then, I get a genuine smile. The first one I have seen, since Kade left.

"That sounds perfect!" She says.

With one last look in the mirror, I head out of my room and towards the lobby, running into Jasper, before I get there. He blocks my way in the staff hallway by the kitchen, and eyes me up and down.

"Where are you going all dolled up like that?" He asks.

He's been here for a few weeks now, and I'd say we tolerate each other. We tend to keep our distance, and I stay out of the kitchen, as much as possible. It works, but I still haven't held a single interview, because he finds something wrong with each one. I'm running out of applicants, and I'm about to go behind his back and hire someone.

But I push that irritation aside and smile.

"I have a date," I say.

Rage crosses his face, but before I can say anything, he gets his emotions back under control.

"Will you have two slices of that chocolate cake left? I promised Lin a girl's night, when I get back." I tell him.

His face softens at the mention of Lin. I confessed to him a few nights ago that she and Kade's relationship started out fake, but then turned serious fast. He's had a soft spot in trying to help her recover ever since.

"How is she?" He asks.

"Trying to pretend she isn't as sad as she is, hence, the chocolate cake."

"I'll put it in the fridge." He says, and then steps aside.

Without another word, I head into the lobby to meet Daniel. He's pretty easy on the eyes, dressed in dark jeans and a button-up shirt. I smile at him, but his eyes dart over my shoulder. When I turn around, I find Jasper behind me.

"Hey, I'm Jasper, the chef here at Sunset." He says and holds his hand out to Daniel.

"I'm Dan." He says.

"Jasper is the *temporary* chef here." I give him a pointed stare.

"Sorry I kept her, had a few kitchen issues to make her aware of, before she left. Enjoy your date and beware of flying fruit." Jasper smirks, and I'm very proud of my self-control for not hitting him with my purse, like I want, too.

I turn to Daniel and smile. "Shall we?" I ask.

I follow him out to his car, and of course, the restaurant he takes me to is Samuel's Southern Seafood, one of Jasper's restaurants. I can't help but laugh, when we pull up.

He looks at me with a confused look on his face.

"Is this okay? It's always been my favorite, but we can go somewhere else." He says, looking unsure.

I place my hand gently on his arm to reassure him.

"It's fine, I promise. The Jasper you just met. Well, this is his dad's place, and now his place I guess, since his dad passed."

Dan's eyes go big. "That's Jasper? Why is he working at your place?"

"Let's go inside, and I'll tell you all about it."

The food is good as always, but I find myself not eating much, because Daniel is just so boring. I want the date over as soon as possible, and when Lin texts me the agreed upon text at the agreed upon time, I'm thankful for the out.

I pull out my phone to check it.

"Sorry, it's just we are short staffed, and with Jasper helping out, I need to make sure everything is okay," I tell Daniel, as I pull out my phone.

"I understand." He says, and then launches into some story about helping his parents, during the season. I type back to Lin about how boring he is, and she sends me back laughing face emojis.

"Daniel, I hate to have to do this, but we need to get back. There's an issue with the sales system." I tell him.

He doesn't need to know we just replaced it, because of the issues we were having, but it's always been my go to, when I need an out of any situation.

"Oh, of course." He says.

I offer to pay my half, but he won't let me, so there's that at least. The entire way home he tells me about the time the sales system went down at the pharmacy.

"I hope to see you again soon." He says, once we are back at The Inn.

"Yes, maybe. With the season coming up, I know we will both be busy." I tell him.

He doesn't try to kiss me, so he gets another point, and I hurry inside, before he can launch into another story.

I make a beeline for the kitchen, because now that the boring stories have stopped, I'm suddenly starving. Unfortunately,

Jasper is still there, wrapping up for the night.

"What are the chances I can bribe you into making me a burger?" I ask him, as I sit on one of the freezer chests. It's something I haven't done in a long time. I'd always sit here, when my dad was in the kitchen talking business. He'd normally give me a Popsicle or some ice cream to keep me busy.

"Didn't he feed you on that date?" He smirks.

"I guess, but I wasn't hungry, then."

"Food suck? Where did he take you?" He asks still a bit cocky, so I decide to take him down a peg.

"Kinda. I mean, he did take me to Samuel's after all." I bite back my smile.

Jasper drops the meat he pulled out for my burger and turns to stare at me.

"What?" He asks and raises an eyebrow at me.

I can't help but burst out laughing. I decide to go easy on him, but I just don't want to tell him how boring the date was. Let him think Daniel is the new love of my life.

"The food was good. I just wanted a burger, and then Lin texted, and so we cut it a bit short. You saved the cake, right?" I ask.

"Yeah, it's in the prep fridge." He nods his head to the fridge on my right.

He turns back to making my burger, but doesn't look at me again, which allows me to take him in. I've never gotten to experience Jasper as a chef. I've seen him in his kitchen, when we were growing up, once he started helping his dad, but he wasn't as confident then, as he is now.

Just watching how seamlessly he manages the grill, while chopping up the lettuce and tomatoes for my burger, is actually

48

a turn on. Who knew?

"Will you be seeing him again?" Jasper asks.

I detect a hint of jealousy in his voice, making me smile.

"Maybe. We both know the season is coming up, and he'll be helping his parents at the shop this summer." I tell him.

"He's a local? Who are his parents?" Jasper asks.

I forget he's been away for a while, and he doesn't know everyone, like he used, too.

"He's Joe and Martha's son. He's going to school to be a pharmacist and take over from his dad." I tell him.

Jasper sets his knife down and leans on the counter.

"Isn't he a little young for you? He was three grades behind us in school."

"Well, slim pickings on The Island lately and all. Everyone is so desperate to see me happy, and since Lin set this one up, and she needs a distraction, I agreed. He wasn't so bad." I shrug.

Let him stew on it. It will do him some good. He plates my burger without saying anything else.

"Do you know if Lin had dinner?" I ask.

"Yeah, I sent a burger to her. She's in your room." He says his tone short.

"Thank you," I say, as I grab a tray and fill it with my burger, the cake, a bottle of wine, and some sodas.

Jasper eyes the tray, but doesn't say anything, as I walk out and make my way to my room.

With my hands full, I can't reach my key, so I knock with my foot calling out, "Room service!"

Lin opens the door with a giggle, and I place the tray on the coffee table.

"Give me five minutes to change, and then I'll give you all

49

the details, but the juicy ones happened after the date!"

Recounting my boring date, and my encounter with Jasper afterwards, seems to spark some life back into Lin. So for that, it was all worth it. I hope her heartache heals soon.

If only I knew the next heartache would be mine, I might have done things differently.

Chapter 8

Jasper

If Brynn can go out on a date, then so can I. When I was making my rounds in the dining room last night, a girl at a table called me over. We got to talking, and they were all friends and meet up once a year here at Sunset to catch up on life, since they all went different ways after college.

One of the girls asked me to dinner. She will be here for a few more days, so I said sure why not. So tonight, she and I are having dinner in The Sunset dining room. My mom wasn't too happy, when she found out, but she didn't say anything. It was just the look she gave me. It's the *'you're doing something stupid, but I'm going to let you do it and learn the hard way'* look.

As I sit across from Jill, I find myself stuck in my old pattern of comparing her to Brynn. Her hair is blonde, and I like Brynn's dark brown. Where Brynn's hazel-green eyes sparkle full of life, Jill's seem coy and calculating. Jill's giggles are so fake and nothing like the sweet melody of Brynn's real giggles. Her dress reveals way too much cleavage, unlike Brynn, who doesn't feel the need to show it all off.

The conversation isn't bad, but she doesn't stop talking

about herself. She's a nurse and grew up in Nebraska, hated small-town life, and loves her city condo. She's the exact opposite of Brynn, and I cringe at the thought of it.

She orders a salad. Of all the amazing dishes I put on the menu, she orders a salad. Brynn would have ordered steak, or fried chicken, or whatever the newest item I put on the menu was. She isn't afraid to dive into a burger and calls a salad a nice snack.

"So, do you have any family nearby?" Jill asks.

"Yeah, my mom lives on The Island. My dad passed away last year, and I'm an only child," I tell her.

Then, it happens. The worst thing she could have done. "Oh, my gosh. I'm sorry about your dad." She says with the biggest fake frown I've ever seen. She reaches out to hold my hand, and I hate the phoney sympathy people try to give. Just be real, you didn't know my dad. It's fine, but don't act like I'm broken, and you have to be depressed over it.

To make matters worse, this is the moment Brynn walks into the dining room, and she sees us with Jill's hand in mine, and her gushing all over me.

I will never forget the hurt that crosses her face, before she turns around and walks back out. My heart clenches, and I immediately feel guilty for being here. I'm such an idiot. This is the lesson my mom knew I'd learn. What was I thinking?

I know what I was thinking. I was pissed that she went on that date with Daniel the other night and wanted to get back at her, and show her I can date, too.

Since Jill's back is to the kitchen, I play the one card I can.

"I'm so sorry. One of my guys just flagged me to the kitchen. There's something wrong. I need to get a check on them." I tell her.

"Oh, of course. Don't worry about me. I'm going to enjoy this amazing meal." She smiles.

I try to smile back, as I head into the kitchen. Thankfully, Ken is there.

"The girl that's at my table? Her meal is on me, send her a dessert, and tell her I can't make it back, and get her out of here. Please."

"Mmm, hmm" Ken answers, and one look tells me he isn't happy.

"Not you, too." I groan.

"Men are such idiots, aren't they? In one night, you do more damage than the last five years combined. You just like digging that hole you're in, huh? Pretty soon you'll be too deep to get back out." He says, heading back to the dining room, knowing I won't follow him.

I rub my hand down my face, because I know he's right.

I head to Brynn's room and pound on the door.

"Brynn, let me in," I say, but the lights are off, and there's no noise or movement from inside.

I make my way over to The Sunrise. My guess is she went straight to Lin. But I make it no further than the lobby, before Dale, the security guard, stops me.

"You looking for Brynn?" He asks.

"Yeah, she come in here?" I ask.

"She did, but I think it's best you let her calm down. She wasn't just upset, she was mad. I haven't seen her like that in a while. I learned early on, when women get like that, you need to let them calm down, before you talk to them."

I take a deep breath. Knowing she's safe at least, I nod to Dale and turn to go home. Today, was my day off at The Inn anyway, and the guys have it covered without me.

The night air is refreshing, as I try to sort out why I feel so damn guilty for going on this date. Brynn went on a date, so why was it okay for her and not for me? Granted, I didn't have to watch her on the date, and I don't know what I would have done if I had. I don't think I'd have been as graceful as Brynn. I probably would have caused a huge scene and put a stop to it.

I walk into the house, and Mom is up waiting on me. With her reading glasses perched low on her nose, as she reads her book on the couch.

"How was your *date*?" She asks.

"Horrible," I say and collapse on the couch beside her, stretching my legs out in front of me.

"Serves you right." She nods.

"Not even going to ask me why it was horrible?" I ask.

She gives me a look, like she knows exactly why it was so bad, and then sighs.

"Why was it horrible?" She asks, but I know it's only because I told her, too.

"Because she was so fake, and then Brynn walked in, and I could tell she was hurt, and she left and went to Lin's. I haven't been able to talk to her."

Mom is so quick I don't even see her move, until she's hitting me with her book.

"You're an even bigger idiot than your father!" She yells at me, but she doesn't raise her voice. How she does that, I will never know. I guess, it's a mom thing.

"What?" I ask her.

"I got tired of waiting for your father to ask me out on a date. So, when a guy from the football team asked me, I said yes. We went on one date, and then went to homecoming together.

Your father was so upset I went on a date with someone else that instead of asking me out, when I broke up with the other guy, he went out with another girl for three months. By the time they broke up, I was dating someone else, and was as angry as a hornet in a cake can and over him."

"I don't remember this part of the story," I tell her.

"It's not our finest moment. I broke up with the other guy at the end of the school year. All summer your dad tried to get me to go out with him, but I was angry and hurt. He spent all summer making it up to me and all senior year too, and I finally agreed to be his prom date with the understanding he wasn't getting any that night." Mom winks at me.

"Ugh, gross, Mom. I don't need bedroom details." I cringe.

My parents were always like this. They overshared their relationships. I know they were each other's first and only, something that while cute, a kid should never know about their parents.

"Well, tough, so here's another for you. Had he sucked it up junior year and asked me out after homecoming, we could have been dating all that time, and he would have gotten some at prom. A fact I reminded him of his whole life."

"Ugh." I stand up, heading to the minibar at the back of the room and pouring myself a whiskey.

"You know, we never know how long we have with someone. That extra year together would have been nice knowing he was going to pass so soon." She says much more seriously. "Brynn's parents were lucky to go together. You don't know what the future holds, or how much time you have, Jasper. Stop playing games and grow a set of balls, son."

"Okay, Mom, time for bed. Me and my *balls* are going to my room." I lean over and give her a kiss, before heading to my room to do some thinking.

I know going on the date tonight wasn't a good idea. I made a rule a long time ago not to date tourists. Mostly, because they just want a vacation fling, and also because if we do hit it off, then you have to deal with the long-distance part, and I'm not a fan of that.

So, I know I need to hold to my rule again. No more tourists.

Then, Brynn's face tonight passes through my mind. Paired with Mom's story. Did I just put up the final wall that will keep us apart? Do I want another chance with her?

Without any hesitation, yes, I want another chance.

So, where do I go from here?

I know I'm going to need to help, so my first thought is to go talk to Lin before I even think about approaching Brynn. I've talked to her here and there. We've passed each other at the graveyard, visiting our parents. One time I helped set up for her summer employees' orientation when I found her upset about Kade.

That day I sent her off The Island to take a break and had Brynn fill in for her. She wasn't happy I talked to Lin, but she forgets we all used to be friends. So, I know I will need Lin on my side, if I want a second chance with Brynn.

Then, like I conjured her up from thin air, my phone rings, and Brynn's name flashes across my screen.

"Hey, I was just thinking about you," I answer.

"Hey, yourself. Listen, I need your help, and it's not for me, it's for Lin." She says, but her tone isn't very happy.

God, thank you for working so fast! This sign couldn't be any clearer, and I promise to fix our relationship.

I had no idea God, fate, karma, or whatever you want to call it could work so quickly. But I thought it, and here it is.

"What do you need?" I ask.

"Listen, Kade called, and he's coming to make things right. He wants to surprise Lin with dinner on the beach tomorrow night. I got the setup taken care of, but would you be willing to cook their meal and make it special? Something that isn't on our menu?" She asks.

"Of course. I'll make her anything she wants." I tell her.

"Perfect, I'll text you the details. Oh, and this is a secret, so not a word to anyone." She says and hangs up.

Well, it's a step with her, though a small one. But this is the perfect opening I needed to start talking to Brynn.

A few minutes later, a text comes in with the food to make, time, and other details for tomorrow night.

Chapter 9

Brynn

My best friend is getting married. Kade came in with a grand gesture straight from a movie, which is perfect with him being a movie star and all. He surprised her with the big apology and declaration of love. He followed that up with a candlelit dinner on the beach, where he proposed.

Of course, she said yes. They want to have a small wedding, since both our parents are gone, and Kade is an only child. They plan to get married after this season. Then, in the off season, they are going to renovate her parents' house, which she currently rents out, as a vacation rental in season. Then, they'll live there.

She won't be next door anymore, but I couldn't be happier for her. Someday, when I find my prince charming, I'll renovate my parents' house, and we will be neighbors again. Until then, I have a place to go to get away from The Inn.

That leads up to today. Kade proposed four days ago, and we are already on the mainland wedding dress shopping. This is something Lin says she wants to get picked out, before the season is kicked into high gear, so she can schedule in dress fittings with Martha on The Island.

Martha is Joe's wife, and they own the drugstore. He runs it, and she helps as needed, but her main job is a seamstress, and she's so excited to do Lin's wedding dress.

"Martha said we can do all the fittings at The Inn and even after dinnertime, so work won't be an issue," Lin says, as we pull into this bridal store Martha recommended.

"Okay, we are early to this appointment." Lin unhooks her seatbelt and turns in her seat to face me. "What's bugging you? I can see it, so let's talk and get it out, before we get swallowed up by tulle."

The plus, or maybe, the downside of having a best friend is they can read you like an open book.

"I don't understand why Jasper went on that date with a tourist. He used to have a rule about not dating them." I sigh.

"That's not it." She says. She knows the problem, but she just wants me to say it.

"Why was he on a date at all?" I say.

"Well, you went on a date." She says.

"That you set me up on." I retort back.

"Exactly." She smiles, like a cat that just caught a mouse.

"What?" I say.

Then, she laughs.

"Didn't you say Jasper followed you to the lobby, and then introduced himself to your date?" She asks.

"Yes."

"He was jealous. So, he thought *'oh, if she can date, I can date'* and I bet that girl just happened to ask at the right time, and he said yes. Did you know Dale stopped him from coming after you not long after you came to my room that night?" She says.

"What? Why didn't you tell me?" I ask.

"Would it have mattered?" She shrugs.

That means, he saw me, and he cut the date short. "Why would he do that?"

"He's a guy, and nothing they do makes sense. You need to decide what you want. If you want another chance with him, then grab on to it. If not, make it clear and set him free. We know better than anyone life can change at the drop of a hat. Stop playing games." She says in her no-nonsense voice.

"Fine, let's go get strangled by silks and choked by chiffons and turn you into a princess," I say, hugging her, while making a silent vow to make the rest of the day all about her.

"Oh, you must be Lin!" The blonde with a way too bubbly personality bounces over to us the moment we walk in the door. "I'm Gigi, and I'll be your wedding dress concierge."

Lin smiles then looks at me, and her eyes say, *'Is she for real?'*

"Yes, this is Brynn, my best friend and Maid of Honor." She says, while grabbing my arm tightly, like she feels they're about to suck her into a wedding dress cult.

"Hi, Brynn! Oh, I love that name! Will your mom or the groom's mom be joining you?" She asks.

Just like that, Lin's face crumbles.

"Lin's parents passed away a few years back, and her fiancé's mom won't be joining us this time, but we plan to bring her back, when she comes to town in a few weeks." I take charge of the situation.

Bubbly Barbie's face falls, and I see the hint of an actual person in there.

"I'm so sorry. My parents have passed too, and I'm dreading my wedding without them." She says softly and places a hand on Lin's arm.

A few other salesgirls are standing towards the back of the room, whispering and pointing our way. My guess is they recognize Lin, as Kade Markson's fiancé. We booked the whole store for our appointment to get some privacy, but we used my last name. While Gigi doesn't seem to recognize her, I'm sure her coworkers will fill her in.

It's hard to believe my best friend is marrying a super famous Hollywood movie star. He has the skills and accomplishments of Brad Pitt, Ben Affleck, and Matt Damon, but the looks of Chris Helmsworth and Channing Tatum all rolled into one. *The lucky bitch.*

"Okay, so dresses. Any idea what you like or don't like?" Gigi slips back into her bubbly personality, and I find myself grateful for it.

"Nothing too poofy, and I don't like the mermaid style. We're doing a small beach wedding, so nothing with a long train. I want to do something with lace, because my mother's dress was lace." Lin says.

"Something with a little glitter that will catch in the sunlight on the beach, so all eyes are on her," I add.

"Perfect! I have a few ideas, but why don't you both go look around and pull dresses you like. Let Brynn pull a few dresses she thinks you would like, since she knows you best." Gigi says. "I'm going to get some snacks and champagne ready, so we can celebrate!"

We start walking around the shop, looking at dresses, some with flowers, and some with different color sashes. Some look like they should have stayed in the 80's.

We split off at one point and walk around the aisle. I pull a dress, and a salesgirl is right there to take it from me, whisking it to the fitting room for Lin. I'm looking at a dress that might work, when I hear Lin gasp.

"Brynn!" She yells, and I take off running towards the sound of her voice. Millions of thoughts flashing through my mind. Maybe, Kade showed up, or his mom, or all the salesgirls attacked her for autographs. I don't expect to find her with tears falling down her face, staring at a dress.

I take a look at it, and my eyes fill with tears too, as Gigi walks around the corner.

"Is this the dress?" She asks, a bit confused.

"This… This…" Lin is too choked up to talk.

"This looks just like her mom's dress, which isn't wearable. It's white and not ivory, but the cut is the same, and the lace is really close to the original. And the belt is different." I whisper.

It has the flowy bell sleeves, the high neckline with a v-cut, and an A-line waist. From the waist, it flows naturally with minimal poof. It used to be called a hippie style dress, but now, it's called boho. Her mom was very much a free spirit, and it fit her personality perfectly.

"Okay, you have to try it on. Right now." Gigi grabs the dress, as I grab Lin, and we head to the fitting room. Gigi and Lin disappear into a room, and I sit on a couch sounded by mirrors.

On the coffee table in front of me, are champagne and little sandwiches. When I take a bite of one, I'm so thankful no one is around to see my face. I don't know if Jasper's food has spoiled me, or if these are truly just horrible, but I barely swallow the bite I took. I turn to the cookies hesitantly, but a small bite confirms they're store bought. Thank God for small favors.

When Lin steps out, she's already crying, and I can't help but cry with her.

"You look just like your mom did in her wedding photos," I tell her.

She stops in front of the three-way mirror and starts swishing side-to-side, as I wait for her to say something.

"It's the perfect dress." She smiles.

"It is." I agree. Then, she looks at the price tag, and her face falls.

"What is it?" I ask.

"It's too expensive." She says, and starts turning back to the fitting room.

"Lin, stop. Think about who you're marrying. Do you think money is an issue?"

"Brynn, it's over ten-thousand dollars!" She says.

"Well, we have payment plans, and I can see what discounts we might have." Gigi tries to help.

"No, I can settle this," I say, pulling out my phone and calling Kade.

"Hey, Brynn. How's it going?" He says.

"She found the perfect dress, and it's the first one she tried on. It's beautiful and looks just like her mom's, but she's refusing to even consider it, because it's over ten-thousand dollars." I tell him, careful not to say his name.

"Put her on the phone." He chuckles.

I hand her the phone, and she walks back in front of the mirror, as they talk, and Gigi turns to me.

"We have some great payment plans, and I can go look. We might be able to sell her that floor model with a huge discount," Gigi says.

I just chuckle.

"Trust me, the money is nothing to her fiancé. It will be fine." I tell her with a smile, but she still looks worried.

I didn't notice the other salesgirl walk up.

"Gigi, don't you recognize her? That's Kade Markson's fiancé." She says.

Gigi's eyes go wide, and she looks over at me.

"Really?" Gigi says.

I laugh, "Yeah, though to me, he's just the annoying guy who will basically be my brother-in-law soon. At least, he's taking over the social media of our businesses off my hands." I try to play it off, but I can tell the girls are dying to ask questions.

"Keep it down, and you can have, until she gets off the phone to ask whatever is on the tips of your tongues," I tell them.

They launch into the same questions we get from everyone. Is he taller/shorter/more handsome in person? What is he like? What did he think playing in this or that movie? How did he propose? How did they meet?

Finally, Lin walks over, and like promised, they clam right up, and she hands me my phone.

"Hello?" I check to see if he's still there.

"She's getting the dress. You have the card I gave you, right?" Kade asks.

"Yep. I'm glad she's getting this dress. It's perfect." I tell him.

"Use the card for the dress. Also, make sure she gets a veil, shoes, and whatever else she needs or wants. Then, take her out to lunch, and go shopping for anything else she wants, okay?"

"I promise to spend as much of your money as I can get her to spend today," I say laughing.

He laughs, too. "Thank you, Brynn. For everything."

"Anything for her," I tell him, and we say our goodbyes.

"Okay, the dress is a go. Do you want a veil, or one of the flower crowns, like your mom used?" I ask Lin.

"Flower crown." She says.

"Okay, shoes?" I ask.

"Barefoot on the beach and flats at the reception."

"God, you're easy." I chuckle.

"What does she need for under the dress?" I ask Gigi.

We walk out an hour later, after Lin has been sized, and they order the dress. When the dress is ready to be picked up, Kade's mom will be in town, so the timing is perfect. We head out to lunch and to look at wedding decorations, like I promised Kade I would. It's one of the best days I can remember the two of us having in a long time.

Chapter 10

Jasper

Lin and Brynn have been out all day. They went wedding dress shopping for Lin, and when Brynn came back, she had a huge smile on her face. God, that smile could get me to do anything in the world. If she only knew the power she had with it, but I'm thankful that right now, she has no idea.

Needing some fresh air, I decide to take a walk along the beach, as the sun was setting. I'm going to figure out how to make things right. Although, I know it won't be easy.

Like the universe is throwing it in my face again, I find Lin, sitting on the back porch of The Sunrise Inn, as I make my way up there.

"Hey," she says, when I reach the steps.

Kade comes out and sits beside Lin on the couch, and I take the chair next to them.

"I'm sorry," I say.

"For?" Lin asks.

"For everything. For blaming you for Brynn and me breaking up, for the way I treated you that night at Samuel's, when you two came in for dinner, for not being here, when your parents died, and for being a shitty friend. All of it." I say.

When I remember that night at Samuel's, I cringe. It was Lin and Kade's first date. Since they were fake dating at the time, they made it very public, and I heard they were at my restaurant and came out guns blazing. Surprisingly, the next day no one was talking about my outburst, just about Lin and Kade. Thank God for small miracles.

She still hasn't said anything, so I keep talking. "When I left for New York, I really thought she'd follow me within a few weeks. Then, her dad died, and she still didn't come. I kept waiting, and the longer she didn't come, the madder I got."

"You know, she was waiting on you, too. Kept thinking you'd show up and apologize. Even after the funeral, she thought you'd realize she couldn't leave, and you'd show up. That you two would get to live out this dream you're now forcing on her by sabotaging every interview she tries to do." Lin says in a very calm and steady voice.

"None of them are good enough," I mumble.

Kade chuckles but stays silent. He wraps his arm around Lin's shoulder, and she rests her head there with her golden, blonde hair, falling down between them.

"So, what's your plan?" She asks.

"My plan?"

"Well, I'm guessing you want me to help you win her back, which is why, you're here. I'm on board, but you have to have a plan. You hurt her by going on that date the other night. More than she wants to admit. As for her date, I set that up weeks ago, before I knew what was going on with you two. It was an attempt to get the heat off me, before Kade and I went public." She says.

Somehow, that makes me feel a bit better that the date was

a setup.

"Also, the date went bad. She was bored out of her mind." Lin smiles.

"Good." I nod.

That explains why she was so hungry that night. Most people, when they get bored, will eat to fill the time. Not Brynn. She can't eat, when she's bored, and it's like her whole body shuts down. I don't know why I bought her excuses so easily. I guess, I was just too mad to see otherwise.

"Now, why did you go on your date?" Lin asks.

"Because I was jealous Brynn went on a date. Trust me, I paid the price and was reminded why the *'don't date tourists'* rule is in place." I shiver, and both Lin and Kade laugh.

I spend a minute and recount the night for them, so they have the entire story, because I'm sure Brynn gave them her side.

"So, you have feelings for her?" Lin asks.

"Always have," I admit.

"You want another chance?" Lin asks.

"Yes." No hesitation. That's exactly what I want.

Before the talk with my mom the other night, I might not have been able to admit it, but my mom is right. You don't know how long you have with the other person, so why dance around it. I want Brynn. I always have, and I think I always will.

"You're sabotaging her interviews, so you have a reason to stick around?" She guesses, even though it's more of a statement.

"I wasn't intentionally at first, but yeah, recently I have been," I smirk.

"So tomorrow, we start the work and planning with the

contractor for the luxury villas we're going to put up across the street. Brynn will be with us all day. Maybe, you could bring us lunch, and while there, give us some ideas." Lin says.

"I'd like that. You can tell me more about the villas, though. I've only heard about them in passing. But tomorrow, will give me a good reason to stay around longer." I wink.

"Mrs. Keller!" Lin says and sits up straight.

I look around for the old lady, but I see no one in sight.

"What?" Kade and I both ask confused.

"I've been trying to figure out who will walk me down the aisle, and I think it should be Mrs. Keller. Think about it. She helped out, after my parents died, she babysat me growing up, and was like a grandma to me. Besides Brynn, she's the closest thing to family I have. I was thinking of asking Brynn to do it, but she's also the Maid of Honor, so I was looking for someone else. Yes, I think it should be Mrs. Keller." Lin nods.

I know that nod. It's the nod that says she's set in her decision, and no one will change her mind, so don't even bother trying.

"That's a perfect choice." I agree with her.

Kade leans over and kisses her temple. "We can go talk to her tomorrow."

"How's wedding planning going?" I ask them.

"Perfect! We got the dress today, and the wedding will take place right here on the beach. Of course, you're catering, and you don't have a choice now." Lin smiles.

"I'd be mad if you went with anyone else," I tell her.

Even if Brynn and I weren't talking, I'd be here ready to cater her wedding. Lin and I were friends growing up, and I had always planned to cater it. Though, I had thought my dad would be by my side for it.

"Well, I'm going to go relay that to my mom, or she'll be mad at me, if she hears it from anyone else." I laugh.

"Of course. Tell her she's welcome at my bridal fitting, and I'll let her know the date, when I have it." Lin says.

"She'll love that." I nod.

I stand to go, and Lin gives me a hug, which I can tell makes Kade a little uneasy.

"Just be patient with her. She's built up a lot of walls in the last five years, and it will take a while to break them down." Lin says.

"I know." I sigh and wave, before turning to walk down the beach.

I've been walking to and from The Sunset each day, so I can take in the water and give myself some thinking time. Today, is no different. I have a lot to figure out, like how I can win Brynn back. By the time I get home, I'm no closer to working it out than I was before.

I find my mom in the same spot, as every night, when I get home. On the couch, reading one of her romance books. So, I sit down next to her.

"I have the latest on Lin's wedding for you." I bribe her to put the book down.

I don't think I've seen this woman move so fast. She sets the book down on the coffee table and turns to face me.

"Out with it, boy!" She says, removing her reading glasses.

"They're having a small wedding on the beach in front of The Inns. It's being catered by yours truly. Lin got her dress today, but I wasn't able to get the details on it, because Kade was there. And she decided to ask Mrs. Keller to walk her down the aisle. Now, you keep that to yourself, until tomorrow and let Lin get a chance to ask her." I say.

"Oh, that's a good choice. Did you hear what she did to the reporter that was hiding in Lin's tree?" Mom asks, shaking her head.

We have all heard this story. A reporter was hiding up in a tree in Lin's property, trying to get photos. Mrs. Keller came out and shot him with her BB gun. He fell from the tree, and she marched over and started cursing him out and stomped on his camera. They ran him out of town with the help of the sheriff.

"That woman stepped up to help Lin, after the accident," Mom says, still lost in thought.

Lin and Brynn's parents were best friends and did everything together. They opened The Inns together next door to each other, bought houses next door to each other, got pregnant together, and sadly, died together.

Five years ago, a freak storm came out of nowhere. Their parents were on a date out fishing, when the boat capsized. Sadly, none of them survived.

"Just like you were there for Brynn. Did I ever thank you for that?" I ask her.

She waves her hand at me and tries to hide the tears, forming in her eyes.

"I mean it, Mom. I wasn't in the headspace to help her the way she needed, but it means a lot to me that you and Dad did. There's a lot I'd do differently, if I knew then, what I know now. How you put up with me I'll never know." I joke, leaning in to give her a hug.

"Lord only knows," she sighs. "You can thank me by fixing things with that girl. Your father and I knew from the beginning you were meant to be, but it just wasn't your time. Maybe now, it is."

"I hope so. I talked with Lin, and she offered me an olive branch. I'm going to take it. Oh, before I forget, Lin wants you at her dress fitting with Kade's mom, and she'll let you know, once her dress gets in." I tell her.

"Oh, I can't wait to see her! Oh, off with you, it's time to go to bed." She says, grabbing her book and standing up.

I hope tomorrow I can start mending bridges and knocking down Brynn's walls.

Heaven help me.

Chapter 11

Brynn

As I stand and look at the property Kade bought across the street from The Inn's, I'm still in shock. Lin and I had been trying to buy this property for years, and the owner was too stubborn to sell. I guess, being able to say they sold it to a Hollywood movie star, changes things.

Since The Inns are at the southern end of The Island, we now basically own the southern tip and have almost doubled our beach space.

"Kade!" I say, as that thought crosses my mind.

"Yeah?" He turns to me all while keeping his arm firmly around Lin's waist.

"You own the beach there!" I say.

"No, we own the beach there. You get a percentage of the villas."

Wait, what?

"Okay, we'll come back to that in a minute. But if you own the beach, does that mean we can do The Sunset events there?"

"Sure does."

"Oh my, gosh, Lin!" I run over and hug her.

"I'm surprised it took you this long to put that together." She says and hugs me back.

"What's all the fuss about?" The gravelly voice I'd know anywhere says.

"Nothing that concerns you," I tell Jasper.

"Brynn just realized, since we now own the land, she can do The Sunset events here," Lin says.

"Better than the roof." He says, as his eyes run over my body, sending a tingle I don't want to admit, too.

I want to be mad, but he's right. Our parents started The Chasing the Sun event, when they built The Inn's. It's why Lin's is named Sunrise and mine is named Sunset. Lin's Inn handles all things morning related, including breakfast for both Inns and a sunrise event on the beach in the morning, during the season. It works out, because Lin is very much a morning person, and now, so is Kade.

I have all things evening, including dinner and a sunset watching event. Until now, we had to do the event on the roof of The Inn, because the owner of the land made it very clear we were not to step foot on it. Even though, it was cleared, and he didn't live on The Island, we didn't want to chance it.

"Oh, I need to re-plan the event and redo the programs, change the website, and get some photos." I pull out my phone, making a list of things to do.

"Well, that's what we're doing today. We're going to meet the contractor to make plans. While I wish the villas could be open for this season, it's not going to happen, but they will be for next season." Kade says.

"Okay, now let's talk about this percentage thing." I level my gaze on Kade.

"Listen, we all know you'll be doing the PR, and this is an

extension of The Inns. So, The Sunset gets fifty percent, and so does The Sunrise."

"Only if you let me pay for half the land, then," I tell him.

"Nope, that's a deal breaker. I bought it to win Lin back, which you helped in by the way. Plus, you'll earn sweat equity on it, and we both know that." Kade says.

It just seems too easy. I turn to look out over the property and right out to the water. This means so much more to me than he could know. This was my mom's dream to host The Sunset events here. I try to get my emotions in check, when Jasper steps up beside me.

He doesn't say anything, just stands there. He knows what this would have meant to my mom, and having him here, is comforting, even if I won't admit that to him.

"I was thinking that they should be called Chasing the Sun Villas," Kade says.

That's when I lose it. I turn and head right for him, pulling him in for a hug. He tenses for a minute, and then hugs me. I pull back, but he keeps an arm over my shoulder, and pulls Lin back to his other side.

"I think today he officially joined the family," I tell Lin, who has a huge smile on her face.

"He sure did." She grins up at him.

The love those two share in just a look makes me so happy for them, and so jealous at the same time, because I want that so bad.

Thankfully, that's when the contractor shows up.

"Brady!" I yell, when I see him.

"Miss Brynn, Miss Lin, I was excited to hear you finally got this property," Brady says.

Brady has been doing work on The Inns for years. His

dad built The Inns, and when he took over, we used him for renovations, after the big storm five years ago, and for little things ever since.

We all chat a bit, but then Kade launches into his ideas, takes in what Brady suggests, and incorporates Lin and my ideas as well. At one point, Jasper disappears, but I'm so involved in the planning, I figure he just went back to the kitchen.

At the end of the meeting, we have decided on eight one-bedroom villas, four with waterfront views, and four behind them with partial waterfront views. We also have two that are two bedrooms, one that is waterfront, and one that isn't.

We agree we want each to have a tropical beach theme, but to be different than the others. But we want them more luxurious than the suites at The Inn. With Kade's name attached to it, he's pretty sure he can get some high-class guests to shell out good money for them. Apparently, he already has several people wanting to come to stay, once they're up and going.

We're just finishing our planning, when Jasper and some of the kitchen staff shows up with lunch and some blankets.

"I thought we'd have a picnic lunch, but it's only right you three have the first meal on the property." He smiles.

"You should join us," Lin says, and I shoot her a glare that she pretends to ignore.

"Don't mind if I do." He says.

He and Kade set up the blankets and food.

We start talking about landscaping, and how to make each villa feel private, and the logistics of bringing food to them from The Sunset kitchen, and all the fun details it's too early to really worry about.

The more we talk, the more I see it and want it.

"You know, I talked to Lin last night," Jasper says, once Kade and Lin start talking amongst themselves.

"About what?" I ask.

"I apologized to her for the way I treated her. I wanted to make things right with her, and figured it would be easy to start there, because I know you won't make things easy on me." He smirks.

"Why should I?" I ask.

"You shouldn't, because I screwed up. I was stupid and had this idea that you needed to come after me, when it should have been me, coming after you." He says.

I can't swallow the lump in my throat, so I say nothing.

"Be warned, Brynn. I'm coming after you now." He leans in and whispers into my ear, causing my whole body to shiver, one I feel right to my core.

Just then, a car pulls up and a door slams. We all turn to find Mayor Jones, heading right to us.

We all stand up, and the guys step in front of us to stop him, before he can get to us. I look over at Lin, who just shrugs her shoulder at me.

The mayor stops short, when he sees the guys, who are taller than him at over six feet to his barely five foot-six-inch frame.

"Really, girls? Bodyguards?" The mayor huffs out.

"Not bodyguards." Kade grits out.

"Now listen here. I just got this letter from the state saying all permits on Main Street have been frozen, because it's under review from the state's historical committee. You're the only two I can think of to do something so stupid!" The man raises his voice.

Both men clench their fists, and Lin places a hand on Kade's arms, making him relax a fraction. I do the same to Jasper, and he looks over his shoulder at me, his eyes soft for me. This is what I wanted, right? What Lin has? Looks like I'm getting it, but it's the absolute last thing I expected.

I put that thought aside to think about later, and push my way between the two guys, so I'm face-to-face with the mayor.

"We talked to you, and Lin talked to you. We gave you the stats, and you ignored them. No one in town wants this, so why do you keep pushing it?" I tell him.

"Because it's what's best for the town. We have to grow and look towards the future." He spits out.

"Are you aware that the last three towns that development was brought into over fifty percent of the year around residents have left? That means fifty percent less taxes for your town. Also, in those towns, after the initial spike of interest, the tourism has started to decline. The regulars stopped going and actually wrote nasty reviews about the development. The developer is about to pull out of one town, because they're barely breaking even anymore. What do you think happens, when they do?" Kade says.

The mayor glares at him.

"I can tell you," Jasper says. "The town dies, it dries up, the last people there leave, and it's the next ghost town. Tourists visiting a decade from now wonder who the idiot was that destroyed the beautiful beach town."

"I've done my research, and they have more successes than failures, mind you. But to make my point clear, as long as permits are halted on Main Street, so will yours for this project." The major spits out.

"Maybe, you should hold a town meeting and let the town vote whether they want the villas, or if they want the development downtown. Or are you too scared you'll be outnumbered, Mayor?"

"Do you think the people in Orlando wanted Disney? But look what it did for that town!" The mayor says.

"Yes, it became overrun with tourism and crime, killed the local flora and fauna, and destroyed historical sites. They tore them down and built over them. The people of Detroit were promised all these jobs from Ford and look where the city is now." I tell him.

"Remember, Mayor, you're an elected official, and only hold the position, as long as the town thinks you have their best interests at heart." Lin reminds him.

"I ran unopposed last time." He waves his hand.

"You won't this time," Kade says.

"What?" The mayor narrows his eyes at him.

"If no one steps up to run against you, then I will. I can guarantee I'll win, too." Kade smirks.

"Go ahead and hold up our permits, we're still winning, because you can't touch Main Street. Remember, we're watching, and if you go against the state's orders, that means jail time." I smile sweetly at him.

"Now, I'm going to have to ask you to get off my property," Kade says, pushing both Lin and me back behind him and Jasper.

The mayor purses his lips, "This isn't over." He says, as he turns on his heel and stomps back to his car.

We all watch him leave. Then, Kade turns and pulls Lin into his arms, kissing the top of her head. Jasper turns to me, and I can see the fight in his eyes. He wants to pull me in for a hug too, and because I could use one right now, I reach for him. He wraps his arms around me and holds me tight. I try to forget the past and remember the last time I was in his arms.

That was the last time I truly felt safe, like everything was going to be okay, and it was, before my parents died. The same feelings wash over me now, like the outside world can't touch me here in his arms. It's dangerous to let my walls down like this; to trust him again, but it can't hurt just for a minute, right?

"I'll fix this, don't you worry," Kade says, and I know he will. He isn't afraid to pull strings if needed to get what he wants.

Chapter 12

Jasper

It's become a routine for me that after the dinner service I go for a walk on the beach. After being in the hot kitchen all night, the waves seem soothing. I don't normally find Brynn sitting on the beach, though.

So, I walk over and sit down beside her. She doesn't move, turn towards me, or speak.

"What are you thinking about so hard over there?" I ask her.

"My parents. I wonder what they would think about all this. About Lin and me fighting to save Main Street, about the villas, you working in the kitchen, and how Lin and me are doing with The Inns. I wonder how my dad would have reacted to Kade, though, I know my mom would be gushing over him. She'd be in heaven right now, planning the wedding with Lin's mom. Can you imagine? She'd decorate the whole town." She smiles.

I can see it all, too. The first time I stepped foot in Sunrise, after being back from New York City, I had the same thoughts.

"I know what you mean. When I think about how my dad would feel about me coming home, I know he'd be happy. But can you imagine how he'd have reacted, when Kade stepped foot in his restaurant?"

"He'd have shoved every dish on the menu at him. Then, chase you around with that metal grill spatula for the way you treated them." Brynn laughs.

I cringe, because she's right. My dad loved that spatula. In fact, I have it in my office at the restaurants, because no one uses it anymore. We're quiet for a while, and maybe, some of her defenses dropped, because it seems she needs to build them back up.

"So, how was your date the other night?" She asks.

"Oh, God. It was horrible." I groan.

"Good!" She laughs.

"She ordered a salad! I mean, I'm a chef, I can cook you just about anything you want, you're eating from my kitchen, and you order a salad!"

Brynn is laughing, "Well, it's my kitchen, and you're just borrowing it." She says, when she calms down.

I smile, but again, I don't say anything. If I have it my way, I won't be leaving it, but she doesn't need to know that, yet.

We sit in silence again for ten or fifteen minutes, or it could have been a half hour. It doesn't matter, because I don't care, and just sitting here with her is enough. But I know I need to start mending fences.

"I get what you went through more than ever now. It's why I hesitated in coming home right after Dad died. I was scared to face you." I admit.

"What? Why?" She asks, like I'm crazy.

"Well, the kiwis for one, and I knew I'd have to have this conversation with you, where I admit what an idiot I was, and how I didn't know what I was doing."

I wish I could find the words to convey to her exactly how I feel, but no matter how hard I try, nothing seems right.

"We were younger, dumber. Lin and I didn't get to make all the mistakes you and other people make in their early twenties. We had to grow up much faster." She says.

"And I should have been here for that. I truly am sorry. But I want you to know, it's always been you." I decide to lay it on thick; put it all out on the line. If it doesn't work out, there will be no regrets that I didn't say or do something that might have worked. That's a lesson my dad taught me a long time ago.

"What?" She asks.

"I tried to date, and all I did was compare them to you. Because of that, I haven't had a relationship, since you." I admit.

Her mouth falls open, and she stares at me, like I just sprouted a second head. My eyes are drawn to her mouth, her perfect pink lips, and I remember what her lips felt like on mine all those years ago. I take the moment of stunned silence to lean in and kiss her. She doesn't kiss me back at first, but when she does, it shocks my whole system.

I don't remember our kisses feeling like this, electrifying and life changing. I don't remember ever being so turned on by a kiss. I gently lean her back on to the sand and deepen the kiss, as she wraps her arms around my neck.

I slowly kiss down her neck. "God, Brynn, I've missed you so damn much," I whisper against her skin.

"Jasper," she gasps and grips my shoulders tighter, pulling me closer to her.

My kiss glides back up to her mouth, and we're in a war for dominance, who is going to control the kiss. I let her lead, and when she nips at my bottom lip, I groan and pull away. It's too fast, and I want to take this slow, letting her know this isn't about sex, and this is about her and us.

The moment I pull away, it's like reality washes over her, and she sits up, catching her breath.

I run a hand down the side of her face and lean to kiss her lightly on her lips.

This time, when I pull back, she jumps up.

"Ummm. Well... I... tomorrow..." She says, her eyes hopeful and runs off to The Inn.

I just shake my head, smiling and stay staring at the water.

I don't notice Kade walking up, until he speaks.

"What has you grinning like a fool?" He jokes.

"Ahhh, just making progress with Brynn," I say.

He cocks his head to the side and stares at me.

"You kissed her, huh?" He says.

My smiles grow. "Yeah."

Kade chuckles and sits down beside me.

"Where's Lin?" I ask.

"She kicked me out of the room, so she and my mom could video chat and talk wedding stuff. I told her she had half an hour, so I figured a walk on the beach was in order." He says.

"So, what are your plans with the mayor?" I ask.

"I have a hunch that I can't prove just yet, so I have a guy doing some digging. Something about this development project doesn't seem to be on the up and up. Like I said, I can't prove anything, but it's a gut feeling, and I always go with my gut." He says.

"I remember Mayor Jones, when I was growing up. His family has always been on The Island. He doesn't get along with his dad. Rumors spread his dad was a drunk, but no one ever saw him drink, and Bert never had any marks on him. At least, that's what my mom said." I tell him.

I pause, trying to pull up the memories I have of Bert Jones.

"He went away to school and came back, and my mom said it's like he was a different person. He wasn't angry, but he disowned his father and helped his mom leave him. She's now retired and living in some retirement resort in Florida. His dad left town, and no one has heard from him."

"What did his parents do for work?" Kade asks.

"Ahhh, let's see. His mom was an elementary school teacher, and his dad worked at a factory on the mainland," I tell him.

"What about Bert? What did he do, before he was mayor?" Kade asks.

"He worked at the bank, doing loans, I think. He became mayor, when I was in high school and has been for years now. I don't know if any of this will help you, but maybe, it will."

"No, it's good background, and it gives me a starting point," Kade says. "Did you hear we're moving up the wedding?"

"No, to when?" I ask.

"Two weeks, before the season gets busy." He says.

"Any reason?" I side eye him.

He chuckles, "No Lin is not pregnant, and that's the first thing my mom asked. It's because I don't want to wait, and when the season ends here, harvesting season begins for my parents, and they won't be able to get away, so it makes sense to do it now. Since I can make it happen, why not? So, tell me what you need to make the food happen by, then." He says.

"Just a menu and a guest count. Appetizers, soups, salad, meals, sides. Do you want it to be a sit down or a buffet? Get with Brynn on drinks to be served."

"Okay, that's all part of what Lin is talking to my mom about.

That and I'm sure my mom is holding up every embarrassing photo she has of me." He shakes his head.

"Lin and your mom get along?"

"Yeah. Almost too well." He smiles.

Good. I'm glad Lin is gaining more family, as she doesn't hide how much she misses her parents. I'm sure it's even worse right now with them not around to help plan the wedding, so I'm happy Kade's parents are stepping in.

"Well, I better head home and tell my mom the news. She'll hang me from the tree in the front yard, if she hears it from anyone else."

"Alright, then. We need you to cook for the wedding, so hurry home," Kade says, as we stand up.

He shakes my hand, and I make the walk back to my mom's house.

Like clockwork, she's sitting on the living room couch reading, when I get home.

"You'll want to put your book down for this, Mom," I say and head to the minibar and pour us both a drink.

"Oh, no. You broke out the rum, what is it? Did you kill someone? I think the shovel is still in the shed, but you will have to do the digging." Mom says.

The sad part? She's 100% serious, and she'd help me bury the body, but then, hold it over my head the rest of my life.

"Nothing like that. It's kind of good news, but I know it will stress you out a bit." I tell her.

"Well, out with it, then!" She takes a sip of the rum.

"Lin and Kade moved up their wedding," I tell her.

She pauses mid drink. "To when?"

"Two weeks, and no she isn't pregnant," I add in, because I know that's her next question.

"Two weeks! Bloody good thing that boy is loaded. What made them move it up so soon?" She says.

"Kade said, when the season ends here, harvest season is starting with his parents, so the timing isn't good. They can get away now, and he doesn't want to wait," I say.

Mom takes another sip, and then purses her lips.

"He's doing it for his parents?" She confirms.

"Yes."

"I'm so glad Lin found a good boy like that with his reputation and all." Mom nods. "Does Lin get along with his parents?"

"Yeah, Kade says her and his mom get along too well," I laugh.

"Good. Tomorrow, you'll drive me into work, and I'll help her get the planning in motion. Did they hire a wedding planner?"

"Mom, I don't know, ask them." I groan.

"Ugh, men never get the details. Just like your father." She shakes her head and heads into the kitchen.

She's still mumbling, while opening and closing drawers, and I know she's pulling out a pen and paper to start making a list.

Lord, help Lin and Kade. Heaven and Hell have nothing on Mrs. Adams, when she gets going.

Chapter 13

Brynn

It has been a crazy week. Who knew planning a wedding in two weeks was so much work? Thank God for Jasper's mom. She's a master planner and great with details. Plus, she knows everyone in town, and who does what. She'd ask a question, Lin would answer, and she's had someone in Seaview on it, before you could blink.

The town has been excited to help. Well, almost the whole town, as a few people aren't fans. Like Jessica. I think she's still mad Kade didn't want her, when she made an open pass at him in front of Lin. Then, during their breakup, she confronted Lin in the Sunrise Lobby and caused a scene, and now, has been banned from the property.

Lin and Kade invited the entire town. Any local who wants to come is welcome, and they're opening the wedding and reception up to the guests staying at both Inns, since all but two rooms are yearly regulars.

I'm walking The Inn, like I do every night before bed, and notice a room that's supposed to be empty due to a cancellation, but it has someone in it. So, I head back to the desk and pull up the reservation list, and sure enough, it's still empty.

I peek my head into Rich's office, since he's still here.

"Rich, did you rent out room four to anyone?" I ask.

"No, it's empty, since the cancellation. Why?" He asks.

"Well, I was just down there, and there's someone inside," I say.

"Employees messing around, maybe?" He says.

"Wouldn't be the first time. I'll go clear them out. Will you add that room to the housecleaning rotation, so we can try to rent it out again?"

"Sure thing. Want me to come with you?" He asks.

"Nah, I'll be fine. I'll have security wait in the hall." I tell him.

He nods and gets back to the bookwork. Normally, a front desk manager would work days, but this season with him and Ken being serious, he took an evening shift, so he can work, when Ken does, and he says he likes it, because most everyone is checked in, and he can do the bookkeeping. I really like having here at night, too.

After filling the lobby security guy in, I grab him and have him wait at the end of the hall for me. Taking my master key, I open the door.

Sure enough, someone is here, and there are clothes strewn on the bed. Looks like someone from the kitchen staff. The shower is on, so I know calling out is useless. I march right in and whip back the shower curtain, stunned to find Jasper, standing there naked as the day he was born. Water is running down his tan skin, and my eyes follow without my permission. His cock twitches and is semi hard.

His chuckle causes me to snap my eyes back to his, and he

smirks. "Care to join me?"

"What the... get out and cover up, so we can talk." I say and storm out of the bathroom, because there's no way I can concentrate with his chiseled abs on full display. Much less, with the V that points right to his cock.

While I sit on the bed, the shower turns off, and a minute later Jasper steps out of the bathroom with nothing but a towel around his waist. Drops of water run down his six-pack, and I have to remind myself why I'm angry at him.

"How did you get in here?" He asks.

"I own the place, and I have a master key," I tell him. "Why are you here? This room is supposed to be empty."

"Yeah, I know, and it's why I'm came in. With the wedding next week, I need to stay late, if I'm going to keep up on bookwork, get everything ordered, and do a test run, before the wedding. So, after my shift, I came in here to shower, because the dishwasher boy was trying to help and spilled a whole bucket of dirty mop water on me. It smelled great, as you can imagine. And I don't have time to run home."

"Well, you could have told me. I'd have let you shower in my room, so we didn't have to clean this one again." I sigh.

"Noted for next time I get dirty mop water spilled on me." Jasper says, walking over to a set of clean clothes on the dresser.

"Where did you get the clean ones from?" I ask.

"I learned a long time ago to always keep a few sets of spare clothes at work. Kitchen accidents happy daily. Not to this extent, but I had a whole pot of cold soup spilled on me once at the start of my shift. After having to work twelve hours in those clothes, I always had extras on hand."

Then, without so much as a flinch, he drops the towel, and his toned ass is on full display.

I gasp. "Jasper!"

"I'm getting dressed to get out of here, but you're welcome to watch." He turns and winks at me, once he has his boxers on.

I want to watch him. No, I want to do more than watch. I want to lick the drops of water, running down his chest.

The danger alarm goes off in my head, and I shoot up and run out of the room.

"Brynn!" He calls out, as I bolt right to my room and fall face first onto my bed.

What the hell is wrong with me? This man broke my heart once. I need to stop giving him the ability to do it again, because he will. My body doesn't seem to care though, and it wants me to ride Jasper and take all its anger and hurt out on him.

I text Rich and let him know what happened, and he tells me housekeeping will take care of cleaning it.

I groan again just as there's a knock on my door. I take my time opening it, because I'm pretty sure I know who is on the other side.

Sure enough, it's Jasper. Thankfully, he's all dressed this time.

"You know, you could have stayed. I'm happy to put on a show for you." He winks. "Maybe next time, it will be me taking my clothes off."

"Jasper, don't." I tell him.

His face goes serious. "Okay, I'm sorry. Just bill me for the room. I didn't mean to cause more work for you."

He turns and starts to walk away.

"Jasper?" I call after him.

"Yeah?" He stops and turns back towards me.

"You can use my office, when you stay late. It has a better view than an empty kitchen," I tell him.

He smiles, "Yeah?"

I nod.

"I'll take you up on that. Get some sleep, Firefly." He says softly, using the nickname I haven't heard in a year.

I smile and close the door. Then, I slowly count to two hundred and sneak over to The Sunrise and down to Lin's room.

I knock on the door.

"Lin, it's me. I have a best friend emergency that trumps your wedding stuff!" I call through the door.

I hear some giggles, and the bathroom door shut, before she opens the door.

Her cheeks are flushed, and her hair is slightly a mess.

"Sorry to interrupt," I call out loud enough for Kade to hear me.

"It's okay, but you'll owe us!" Kade calls back.

I smile and collapse on the couch.

"What happened?" Lin says.

"Jasper kissed me," I tell her, starting from the top, because we haven't had time to talk.

"What, again?" She says.

"What do you mean again?" I say.

"Kade told me he kissed you on the beach last week." She says.

"How did Kade know?" I ask.

"Jasper told him." She shrugs.

"He's a bigger gossip than you and me. Okay, no, not again, but I did just see him naked." I say just as Kade walks out.

"Do I need to leave for this, cause if it's sex talk, I'm leaving,"

Kade says.

"No sex talk," I tell him.

"Okay explain, and then start from the top." She says.

So, I tell her about the canceled reservation, finding some-one in the room, about busting in and finding Jasper in the shower, our talk, him dropping the towel, me bolting, and him coming after me.

Lin tries to hold back a smile, but Kade full on laughs so hard that I throw a couch pillow at him, which makes him laugh harder.

"It's a guy's natural reaction to the girl we like, walking in on us naked. We want to show off. Of course, he's going to flirt, and why not? Plus, it's not like you haven't seen it before." Kade shrugs.

"That was years ago. He's changed a lot and gotten some ink." I say, remembering the tattoo, I didn't have time to focus on before.

"Well, I guess the next question is, are you going to give him another chance or not?" Lin says bluntly.

"What?"

She sighs, "Brynn, why do you think he sabotages all the chef interviews? Why is he still here? Why did he kiss you? Why did he flirt, when you saw him naked? Why is he busting his ass to help with my wedding? Why was he protective of you with the mayor? Hell, why do you think he volunteered himself for the job in the first place?"

Honestly, I hadn't wanted to let my head go there just in case I was wrong.

"Do you think?" I ask her.

"We know," Kade says.

I think back to the last few weeks, and it felt right having him in the kitchen. Despite everything, I trusted him there, and if he said we needed to do something, I did it. It felt like he belonged, and it was comforting. That's probably why I didn't fight him too hard on the interviews.

"I can try to be a bit nicer, but I make no promises. Well, I can make you one. Next time, it will be a softer fruit I launch at his head. Because this is Jasper, and you know there will be a next time without a shadow of a doubt." I tell them.

Lin nods, "I can live with that."

I groan. "Stupid me agreed to let him use my office, and I'm pretty sure my porch door is locked. No way I can sneak back to my room."

"Oh, I have your porch door key." Lin jumps up and rummages through her nightstand.

"Here." She says, handing me a key. "Just make sure I get it back, because I see many more nights like this in your future."

We hug, and then, I head out from her back door onto the beach. The dark night and the moon reflecting on the water should be calming to most people, and it used to be to me. Now, it just gives me the creeps. So, I run straight to my room, thankful to see the blinds in my office closed, but the light is on, so I know he's there.

I make it to my room safely this time. I don't think the next time that I will be so lucky.

Chapter 14

Jasper

Tonight, is Kade's bachelor party. By party, I mean a night at The Hummingbird Bar and Grill. This is the other place my family owns, and it has an island feel to it. My dad had fun building this restaurant. We visited many island bars up and down the coast, taking notes of decor and food. He wanted it to be different.

There's a traditional Tiki Bar, but then, there are lots of blue and white painted wood and relaxing chairs around a dance floor. This place has the best burgers in town. The last seven years in a row, it was voted best burger place, so it's not just me saying it. Best of all, if you sit upfront, you get water views. There's some outdoor seating, too.

I thought for such a popular Hollywood movie star that Kade would have a bunch of guys here tonight.

Nope, it's just him, me, and his dad.

"So, are we waiting on the rest of the groupies to get here?" I ask, once we order our drinks.

"Nope, this is it. I know a lot of people, but I don't trust a lot of people. Once I left that life, even my manager dropped contact with me. I can't blame him after walking off a major movie set and breaking my contract to come back here. I told myself to find what made me happy, and this is it. Making money makes him happy, so good for him." Kade says.

"Do you miss it at all? Hollywood, I mean." I ask, as we order our drinks.

"I miss the Mom and Pop Italian place near my house, and I miss some of the shops, but no. When I was there, I missed Lin so much more. I also missed the quiet, the beach, and everyone here." He says.

I can't say I blame him. It was the same way, when I was in New York City. It was too loud and too busy. I missed home, but I had it in my head that to make anything of myself as a chef, that's where I had to be, and where I had to work. Now, the only people's opinions I care about are right here on The Island.

"As much as I wish you'd come home and run the ranch, son, I think you're where you belong. Watching you the last few days, it suits you, and you're happier than you ever were in Hollywood." Kade's dad says.

I shake my head, as I still can't picture Kade growing up on a ranch in some small Midwestern town.

"Plus, now you have no excuse not to come to visit more." Kade jokes.

Kade's parents hated Hollywood and rarely visited him there. They would visit him on set, when he would film on location, and only go to Hollywood for movie premiers or award shows to support him.

"So, what's good to eat here?" Kade's dad asks.

"I don't know, never been here. Ask Jasper, he owns the place." Kade says.

"Is that true?" Kade's dad looks up at me.

"Yeah, my dad opened this one and Samuels Southern Seafood. He was a chef, too. When he passed, my mom ran them for a bit, and I came home to help. Then, Brynn needed help, so I've been there, helping her out. Dad had these places running themselves, but I like to pop in now and then to check on them." I shrug.

"Okay, then you order for us." Kade's dad nods.

"Go with a burger, any burger. It's what I get, when I come here. My dad used to experiment with burgers, and the best ones made it on the menu." I tell them.

We place our order, and then I turn to Kade again.

"So, do you think you will ever do another movie?" I ask.

"Never say never, but I have no plans, too. I've never been happier than I am here. Even when Lin and I fight, it's still better than my best day in LA. Making movies was never my dream. I enjoyed it at first, but not really at the end." He says.

"Good answer. I guess, I should warn you now, since her dad isn't here, and I grew up with the girls, I feel it's only right I give you a hard time. Make sure you're ready to commit." I tell him.

"Bring it on. I'll gladly take anything you can throw at me, because that means Lin has a support system behind her." He smiles.

I don't doubt his feelings for Lin, and I don't doubt how Lin feels about him. I can see how much they love each other, but I don't want to let him off too easily either. He broke her heart, when he left, and I know she has forgiven him, but he still has to pay for that.

"Good. You know it won't stop just because you get married either. The moment you get married, it's like the town will suck you in. You're one of us, but you mess up, and they'll still take Lin's side every time, even if she's wrong." I level with him.

"I've seen the special bond this town has with her. They rally behind her and want what's best for her. I'm okay with that." He smiles and shakes his head. Then, he tilts his head towards the pool table. "Play a round?" He asks.

"He didn't get his pool skills from me. I don't play, so I'll be the judge to make sure you both play fair." His dad says.

"So, what are the girls up to tonight?" I ask him.

"When Brynn found out my mom has never seen *Magic Mike*, that sealed it, and instead of going to a strip club, they're watching strippers on TV. I guess, I prefer that than them going in person," Kade says.

"I will agree with you there," I tell him.

I don't like the idea of Brynn at some sleazy strip club, not one bit. Hell, I don't like the idea of Lin at one either.

"My mom promised not to let them get into too much trouble tonight," Kade says.

"Well, your mom has been known to get into plenty of trouble all on her own, so don't let her sweet talk you there." Kade's dad says.

As the night goes on, we eat, have a few more rounds of drinks, and enjoy the night.

Nate stops by once he gets off duty, and when he walks in the bar with his police uniform on, everyone freezes, waiting to see who's in trouble.

"I'm here off duty, just came to celebrate with the groom." He holds his hands up and laughs.

All in all, it's a pretty easy-going night as far as bachelor parties go. This is how I want my bachelor party to be. Good

98

friends, great food, and some laughs.

* * *

Brynn

"OH MY, GOD!" Kade's mom screams, as the guys on the screen rip off their clothes. "Why haven't I seen this before?"

We are holed up in my room, watching *Magic Mike*, the first and the second one. Jasper made sure the kitchen brought us plenty of food and dessert. I stocked us up with drinks, and we are enjoying the guys on the stage.

"We have to introduce her to *Fifty Shades of Gray* next," I say.

"I'm never going to be able to look her in the eye again." Lin laughs.

"Oh, posh. I was wilder in my younger days. My parents thought I was crazy, when I said I was marrying a rancher and planned to settle down on a ranch in the middle of nowhere. But I knew he was it for me, when I met Kade's dad. It's just like Kade knew, when he met you." She smiles at Lin.

"What kind of trouble did you get into?" I ask.

"Let's see. A few friends and I always had fun sneaking into bars long before we were old enough. We liked to dance and flirt, and we would lead guys on more than we should have. We'd get in boys' cars we didn't know and go for a drive. All the stuff that, as a mom now, makes me cringe." She says.

"Well, as my mom used to say, it was a different time," I tell her.

"That it was. Thank God, because it would be a crime not

to have these lickable men on TV!"

This is how the night goes, until the guys come knocking on the door. It's obvious that we had much more to drink than they did. Kade and his dad help his mom and Lin back over to The Sunrise, and Jasper stays behind, leaning against my door frame.

"You guys have fun?" I ask.

"Yeah, we spent the night at The Hummingbird Bar." He says.

"That's what Lin said."

"Heard you had some fun with *Magic Mike*." He smirks.

I sigh, "That we did. Those two are all worked up for their men now. Care to come in and take care of me?" I ask, before I can even think about stopping the words from leaving my mouth.

His gaze gets heated, as he rakes his eyes down my body and back up again, before stopping on my face.

"How much have you had to drink tonight, Firefly?"

"Enough that I feel good, but not enough to be hungover in the morning."

He reaches out and brushes his thumb along my bottom lip. "I'd love nothing more than to take care of you, but I won't take advantage of you, while you've been drinking." He says.

I shrug, "Okay, just know that I will be taking care of myself tonight."

He groans. "Know I will be cumming multiple times tonight, thinking of you lying in your bed, taking care of yourself."

He kisses my cheek, and then is gone, closing the door behind him.

Damn. Tonight, just got much more exciting.

Chapter 15

Brynn

When Lin and I were kids, we used to play wedding day, just like any young girl would. My mom would let us use her white sheets and make these crazy wedding dresses, and later, we'd use old Halloween costumes.

We'd drag in any boy we could to play our groom. Mostly, it ended up being Jasper and Lin's ex, Travis, back when we were no more than eight or nine.

Then, one day, when we were teens, we snuck into her mom's closet and got out her wedding dress and tried it on. I remember thinking about how much like a bride Lin looked, and how beautiful she was. Of course, her mom found out, and we got in trouble for going into her closet, but not for trying on the dress.

Today, with Lin standing in front of me in her wedding dress, all I can think about is that day she wore her mom's wedding dress. The dress is so similar, but has some twists that are all Lin, like the sparkle belt she added on.

Everyone came together to make this day special for her, and in record time too, thanks to Jasper's mom. We're getting ready in my room at Sunset, and I just finished buttoning Lin into her dress. With her hair and makeup done, I get the full effect and lose my battle of trying not to cry.

Thankfully, we went with waterproof mascara.

"Okay, guests are starting to arrive and being seated, the weather is gorgeous, and Nate and his guys have the road blocked off, so only guests and locals can get anywhere near here. He even has guys patrolling the beach. There are a few boats in the water, so I guess if they had the fancy lens things, they might get some photos." Mrs. Adams says.

We open the bathroom door to a chorus of praise, and how pretty she looks.

"Besides, if they try to get photos from the water, they won't get good ones with the sheer curtains you put up on the arch and the decorations, which was good thinking on your part." Lin reminds her.

"That's true." Mrs. Adams straightens her back and smiles.

"Well, any last-minute details? My husband texted that Kade is pacing the room and driving everyone nuts." Kade's mom laughs.

"Can I have just a minute with her?" I ask.

Everyone nods and heads out to take their spots.

"Okay, this should be your mom doing this, and I know I'm a shitty substitute, and I don't want to make you cry, but here goes nothing," I say, as tears already fill both our eyes.

I walk over to my dresser, and with shaking hands, pull out the little box I had been saving for this day.

"The last date I had with Jasper, before he went to New York, was a special one. Your mom had me convinced he was going to propose. She had me dress up and let me borrow this." I hand her the box.

"I forgot to return it, and the well, you know, and then, I saw it as I was moving out of the house. I swear I heard your mom standing there whispering to save it for you for this day." I tell her.

Her hands shake as badly as mine, when she removes the necklace from the box.

"I've never seen this one before." She says.

"She told me she wore it the day your dad proposed. She said he gave it to her, when they graduated high school, and she wore it the day she was married as well. It was good luck, and I should wear it, too. When I checked the photos, sure enough, she was wearing this necklace. So, I decided to hold on to it and wait."

I barely get my words out, before Lin is launching herself at me and wrapping me up in the biggest hug. It's hard to breathe, but I don't say anything, as I just hug her back as hard.

"I love you, Brynn. You have always been family, and now, our family is growing, I promise to give you plenty of nieces and nephews to spoil the hell out of. We will grow our family and never be alone again." She whispers in my ear.

I choke up, but manage a deep breath, as I pull away, "Maybe, not too soon though, okay?"

She laughs, "Deal. Now, how bad is my makeup?"

"Not bad, let me fix it for you," I tell her.

A few minutes later we head out to the lobby and meet Mrs. Keller, who is walking her down the aisle. Mrs. Adams is there, and she gives us a soft smile.

"You made her cry." She states.

"But I fixed it." I laugh.

She shakes her head and hands both Lin and me bouquets of flowers. I'm her Maid of Honor, and Jasper is Kade's Best

Man. Small wedding, but then, our family is small. Lin's right though, it's growing.

I turn back to Lin right before walking out of the door.

"I want a family so big we barely fit in one house for Christmas," I tell her.

She nods, "We will make it happen."

Then, I'm walking down to the beach, everyone is seated, and all eyes turn to me. Kade and Jasper stand up by the water with Kade's family pastor, who flew in just for the ceremony.

I don't see all the people, and I don't even see Kade. My eyes lock with Jasper and don't leave, as I make my way up the aisle. My mind's screaming that I could have this if I just let him in, if I just let one wall down, give him a sliver of trust, and give it a test run. Open myself up and try.

I take my spot, and then the music changes, and everyone stands, and watches Lin walk onto the beach. I couldn't tell you if Kade cried, or if Lin's eyes stayed on Kade's, because my eyes were still locked with Jasper's.

The entire ceremony we go through the motions, but his eyes never leave mine. During the vows, his gaze gets intense, almost like he's making me the same vows.

It's in this moment that I realize no matter what, it's always been him at the end of the aisle, when I pictured my wedding. The thought freaks me out, and I'm just on this side of a panic attack, when the pastor says, "You may now kiss the bride."

Thankfully, it's a short kiss. Then, they walk back up the aisle with Jasper at my side, as we follow them.

"What went through your mind just then?" He says.

He's always been able to read me, and always knows, when something is wrong.

"Play your cards right, and maybe, I'll tell you." I try to

lighten the mood.

Today, is about Lin and Kade, and I want to be here for them.

We get through pictures and greet just about everyone, before Jasper and I make it to the reception room at Sunrise. The place doesn't look the same. It's beautiful and what Lin called 'Hollywood beach glam.' She wanted to show they were merging their two worlds.

Before I know it, a bottle of water is in front of me.

"Drink up, we were outside for a bit," Jasper says.

"Thank you." Taking the bottle, I drink thirstily. He watches me and nods his approval, when I finish a fourth of the bottle.

We turn to watch Lin and Kade enter the room, and Lin looks at the wall by the door, blushes, and then smiles at Kade. I just know something happened here, and I love that they have those moments together.

The food is set up buffet style, and of course, all of it is Jasper's cooking. He prepared Lin and Kade's favorite foods. We spared no expense for them, as Kade insisted. There's everything from steak, to appeal Kade's parents, local seafood, Jasper's famous dishes, and a few meals to appease some of the townspeople on special diets.

We eat, and then, it's time for speeches.

"I'll go first," Jasper whispers, and then stands up at our table.

Lin and Kade chose to have a sweethearts table, so it's just them. Then, Jasper and me being the only wedding party are at a table to one side, and Kade's parents, Mrs. Adams, and Mrs. Keller are at the parents' table to the other side.

Kade asked Jasper to be his best man, and I was shocked. But Lin said it's because Jasper has always treated him like he was normal. Even grilled him to make sure he was good enough for Lin. He's been the most real friend he's had, since he moved to Hollywood, and that made me happy. Even if it meant I was stuck with Jasper all night.

"I haven't known Kade all that long. In fact, when he came to town, I didn't like him. I didn't want some Hollywood playboy around the girls." He points to Lin, and then to me. "I wasn't very nice to him at the beginning, and for that, I'm sorry," he says to Kade.

"Don't be. It was the first time someone wasn't kissing my ass, and I enjoyed it!" He laughs, and so does the rest of the room.

"But I got to know him, as I watched him with Lin, and what I saw was what I had always hoped for. See Lin, Brynn, and I grew up together, as most of you know. It was the three of us and another old friend, and the four of us were inseparable growing up."

I smile, liking that Jasper doesn't mention Travis, Lin's ex, by name. He's here today, but Kade isn't his biggest fan, though Travis is a huge fan of Kade's.

"What I saw with Kade in the last few months, minus the time the dumb ass went back to Hollywood," he pauses, and everyone chuckles. "Was that he took care of Lin, like she was the most precious thing in the world. He opened his arms to Brynn just because she was important to Lin. Kade taught me a valuable lesson, and it's one my mom has been trying to teach me from Kindergarten. Don't judge a book by its cover. Kade is the exact opposite of what you read in the papers. He's kind, caring, and one of the most real people I have ever met. Somehow, he was able to forgive me for being a total bastard, when we met, and here I stand in front of you today. I'm overjoyed to see how happy they are, and now, I have someone else helping me watch out for these two who seem to always find ways to cause trouble. To Kade and Lin." He holds up his glass, and everyone echoes him, as we all drink.

He sits down and looks at me. My turn. I smile and stand.

"I've had a few sleepless nights trying to figure out what to say today. Lin and I always played wedding as a kid. Later, we roped Jasper into playing the groom." I smile down at him, and again, leaving out Travis.

"It's every girl's dream the special day they get to walk down the aisle." I look at Lin, and her eyes are already starting to water. "Damnit, Lin, I wasn't going to make you cry, but since you are, I'm going to go there," I say, and the room chuckles, and Lin smiles up at Kade.

"Every girl dreams of their dad walking them down the aisle. Five years ago, that dream was ripped from both of us." I say. No explanation needed, as almost everyone in the room lived it with us. The room is so quiet you could hear a pin drop.

"That day forced us to change our dreams. We healed, and Lin dragged me kicking and screaming back to the light with her. One night about two years ago, after season, and after a lot of wine, Lin said to me the same thing I said to her today right before I walked down that aisle. I want a family so big that it doesn't fit in the house at Christmas. For the last five years, the only family we had was each other. So that night, after more wine than I care to admit, she made me promise her something that today Kade has relieved me of." I smile, as Lin's eyes are wide, and Kade is looking at her, like she hung the moon.

"She made me promise that if we weren't married by the time we were thirty, then we'd move into one of our parents' homes and become single moms together. We'd adopt as many kids as we could afford, and we'd build our family anyway. I

107

agreed, because at the time, I thought that would be the only way." I give Lin a wobbly smile, and Jasper reaches over to give my hand a squeeze, and I smile down at him. He offers me a sad smile back.

"So today, I pass the torch to Kade. Our family has grown by one, and I expect a lot of nieces and nephews running around. Kade has made Lin happier than I remember her being in a long time. In one day, she gets a husband, and a mother and father-in-law, and I get the brother that I never wanted."

Kade laughs with a sparkle in his eye.

"I had a front row seat to their love story, and it was better than any movie or book I have read. Nothing beats watching your best friend fall in love. That said, I may not have stepped foot on a boat in five years, but you hurt her? I will charter a boat to the middle of the Atlantic and drop your body, where no one will find it." I level him with a gaze that says, while everyone is laughing, I'm serious.

"I promise to take care of her." He says.

"Good, now I was promised some of Jasper's cake that I haven't had, since we were kids, so let's get this party going!" I yell, and the music kicks on.

I collapse in my chair, feeling like I just ran a marathon. Jasper takes my hand and holds it, rubbing his thumb over the back of my hand.

Then, he leans in to whisper in my ear, "If you stop being so stubborn, you could have this too, you know. Now, dance with me."

The rest of the night is filled with lots of laughter and dancing. The last time Jasper and I danced together was prom, and he's gotten much better. He must see the question in my eyes, because he whispers, "I had to learn ballroom dancing, because the restaurant I worked for was big into charities in town, and my boss made it clear I was to be seen dancing. I never took a date, though."

I hide my smile. This is my Jasper, just so much better.

Chapter 16

Jasper

God, Brynn was so beautiful in that dress she wore at the wedding yesterday. It was a strapless baby blue that was flowy, and when the wind caught it, she looked like a goddess with the flowing dress. It's all I've been able to think about. Her in that dress and in my arms all night.

I walked her back to her room, and I could see the desire in her eyes. It was like the one the night of the bachelor party and like that night she had been drinking. I know she wanted me to kiss her, but I gave her a quick kiss on the cheek and went home. It was so hard, but I need her to open and let me in, even just a little.

We're prepping for dinner, which should be slow, since everyone in town was out yesterday at the wedding, allowing my mind to wander, until the kitchen door opens and in walks Brynn. She isn't in her normal shorts and a tank top. She's wearing cut-off jean shorts that show just a hint of the bottom of her ass cheeks with a button-down shirt with just enough buttons undone to show off her cleavage, and I couldn't turn away from her, even if I tried.

CHAPTER 16

Then, a sharp pain shoots from my finger up my arms. I look down and realize I cut myself.

"Fuck!" I shout and grab the towel from my back pocket, wrapping it around my finger.

I just look at the prep guy next to me, and he starts cleaning it up, as I head back to the office.

"Oh, gosh. Are you okay?" Brynn walks over and takes my hand in hers. "Come on, there's a first aid kit in my office."

I don't stop her to tell her there's a first aid kit in my office in the kitchen. I just follow her to her office. I like the idea of Brynn taking care of me, having her hands on me, and being in her space.

"Here, sit on the couch." She says, pulling a large kit off the bookshelf.

She sits down next to me and sets my hand on her lap. Even though, I can take care of it myself no problem, as I've done it before, I want her to do it. There's just something special about her taking care of me, especially, after the last few nights.

She opens the towel and wipes away the blood, before opening an alcohol pad and cleaning the area up. She doesn't flinch or make a face at the blood. With her hands on me and her sitting so close, I don't feel the cut anymore, and I'm not looking at it, I'm looking at her.

The slight pinch between her eyebrows, as she assesses the cut, is endearing. How she bites her lip, as she concentrates on cleaning the cut up without hurting me, and I love that she's taking care of me. My heart wants to leap out and make her stay and do this every day.

"I don't think you need stitches, and it looks like the bleeding has already stopped." She says, as she applies some cream and a Band-Aid.

111

When she's done, she sets the kit on the floor and turns to look at me, taking my hurt hand gently between the two of hers.

"You have to be more careful," she says tenderly.

I smirk, "You need to be less distracting."

"You're blaming this on me?" She smiles.

"Always. I can't seem to concentrate on anything else, when you're around." I say and lean in a bit more.

Watching her bite her lip, all I can think about is how I want to be biting that lip myself. She leans in, and at the last second, turns and kisses me on the cheek, before she stands up.

"Be careful, and if you want to join me for a beer on the porch after dinner, I will be there." She says and walks out of the office, leaving me staring after her.

That kiss was payback for last night; I know it was.

After dinner that night, I join her on the porch. She knew I would be there, because there was no way I'd miss a chance to spend time with her. She's sitting on the wicker sofa, looking out over the water, as I sit down next to her, so close that our shoulders are touching.

"How's your hand?" She asks.

"A little sore, but good to go. Only a little lettuce was damaged in the process." I tell her and smile.

"I miss having dinner with Lin." She says. I know her and Lin had dinner every night together, no matter what, since they took over The Inns.

"Her and Kade locked in their room?" I ask. Since the season officially kicks off this weekend, they decided to wait and do a honeymoon after season. Kade said he'd take her anywhere she wants to go, so her and Brynn have been plotting and planning.

112

"Yeah, but I can't blame them. I'd spend every minute with my new husband, too." She takes a long pull from her beer, and then grabs one from the side table, handing it to me.

"You should be careful dressing like this," I say and lightly trace the deep cut of her shirt.

Her breathing quickens, as I trace from the low dip in her shirt, back up to her neck, and lightly ghost my hand up her jaw, and then over across her lips, before I pull back. It's a game we're playing to see who can hold out the longest, or who breaks down and kisses who first.

"Why, because it causes guys to attempt to chop their fingers off?" She jokes.

"It gives guys ideas that you might be dressing up for them," I say.

"What if I am?"

"Then they're definitely noticing," I tell her, letting my eyes run over her body.

"You're beautiful, Brynn, and you don't have to go out of your way to make anyone notice that. I see it every day, so don't change to get anyone's attention, because you already have it." I whisper.

Her lips part slightly, and I'm about to say fuck it and kiss her, when she clears her throat and turns back to face the water, as she drinks some more beer.

We talk some more about safe subjects, like the plans for the dinner menu next week, and local town gossip.

"Well, I think we should call it a night." She stands, and I follow her.

"I don't need an escort, you know." She smirks.

"I will always make sure you get to your door. I always did, when we were kids, and I will continue. That hasn't changed."

113

I tell her.

"Good, while I hope something has changed, I hope most of you hasn't." When she reaches her door, she turns, and her eyes rake down my body.

I step in, crowding her and wrap an arm around her waist.

"I've changed in the best possible ways," I whisper against her ear and ghost my lips down her neck, before pulling back.

The frustration in her eyes is clear, and I just smile. "Goodnight, Firefly." I turn and head back to the kitchen, making sure everything is in order, before I start my walk home.

I'm going to need to start driving to work, because there are just too many people on The Island now to enjoy the walk back to my mom's. On the way, I get a text from Kade.

Kade: News says there are storms tomorrow night. Brynn hates storms and can't sleep. Thought you'd like to know.

I read the text over and over, before it hits me. He's giving me a way to get closer and work my way back in.

Me: Thanks, man. I will take care of her, I promise.
Kade: Good. Lin isn't very happy I'm keeping her from Brynn tomorrow night, so make the most of it.
Me: I promise.
Kade: Good luck.

I don't realize I'm smiling so big, until I walk inside, and my mom whistles.

"Looks like you're a cat that caught the canary. Out with it, boy." She says from the kitchen.

"Kade and Lin are doing some matchmaking is all. A little

push towards Brynn." I tell her.

"Well, don't let her dangle too long. The season is starting, so you know she'll use that, as a reason to keep you at arm's length," Mom says.

"What happened to your hand?" She lifts my hand, looking at the bandaging job Brynn did.

Mom unwraps my hand and examines it, before pulling me over to the sink and washing it.

"Ahhh, Brynn distracted me, and I cut myself. Then, she bandaged it up for me."

Mom smiles, and then goes back to the cabinet, grabs her first aid kit, and adds some more cream and a new Band-Aid. I watched her do this for my dad many times, when he'd come home with a new cut or scrape. Once she's done, she washes her hands and goes back to what she was doing.

"You need to be careful. You know at one point, your dad banned me from the kitchen. Said I was too distracting as well." She smiles at me, before turning back and scooping the cookies in front of her into a cookie tin.

"What are these for?" I ask her, trying to change the subject.

I pick up a cookie to eat, when mom slaps my hand with the spatula, and then points the spatula at my face.

"These are for church. Keep your hands off. Now, you give me a daughter-in-law and some grandbabies, and I'll bake you cookies every day. Until then, hands off." She says with a pointed look.

I hold my hands up in surrender. "Okay, and I'm working on it. Lots to make up for, Mom, so it will take time. Oh, and I may not be home tomorrow night. It's supposed to storm."

"What's that have to do with the color of roses?" She asks.

She has been saying that, since I was a kid, and I still don't get the exact meaning, but I know what she's asking.

"Brynn doesn't like storms, so if I get the chance to stay and comfort her, I will." I shrug.

Mom looks at me and narrows her eyes. "Daughter-in-law, and *then* grandbabies. In that order, understand me, mister?" She says, and I just smile.

"Dad gave me the safe sex talk, so you're in the clear." I joke.

"Boy!" She calls after me, as I head down the hall.

"Night, Mom!"

She's just too easy to rile up. What I don't tell my mom is that I'll take Brynn any way I can get her, even if that means babies at the wedding.

Chapter 17

Brynn

I hate thunderstorms. I also hate the fact that Lin has Kade tonight, and they're probably so distracted they don't even realize it's raining. I'm so happy for her, and I want that, too. Because sitting here on the porch alone as the rain, thunder, and lightning fill the sky, isn't very fun.

I consider heading to my room, but I won't be able to concentrate on anything, so here I sit.

When lightning fills the air, I close my eyes and count, until I hear the thunder. It's a game my mom used to play with me.

This is why I don't see Jasper, until he sits down next to me on the porch.

"You okay?" He asks.

"I guess," I sigh, not sure what to say.

"Storms never bothered you before. How many times did you, me, and Lin run up and down that beach in the rain, until your parents yelled at you to come inside?"

"On the night they died, the storm was worse than this and popped out of nowhere. A *'Ghost Storm'* they call it. Now, all I can think about it is the accident. Did they see it and try to

117

make it home in time? Did they suffer? Were they scared? Did one have to watch the other die? Questions I don't want answers to, but still run through my head."

He wraps an arm around me and pulls me into him. I rest my head on his shoulder and just sigh. Peace is what I feel here in this moment.

"Tell me about that night." He says.

Well, the last thing I want to talk about is that night, but okay.

"Mine and Lin's parents went out fishing for the day. The season had just ended, and it was their way to unwind. They asked Lin and me to go, but we wanted to stay home and have a girl's day. We painted our nails, snuck some of my mom's wine, watched movies, bitched about you, and all that fun stuff." I tell him.

He lightly runs his hand up and down my arm.

"The storm came, and they didn't come home. We didn't think much about it, as they would always stay at the docks, after a trip to eat and drink and talk. We assumed they were there and planned to wait out the storm. Come morning, they still weren't home, and neither was the boat."

I remember the sheer panic I felt, when I realized they didn't come home. I close my eyes, as a chill runs through me. Jasper must have felt it, because he pulls me into his lap and wraps both arms around me.

"So, the town went searching. They found the boat not too far from The Island. There were two bodies near the boat, and the other two were found later that day, and Lin and I never asked which was which, as we didn't want to know. So ever since, Lin and I would sit on the porch and snuggle up together during a storm. Now, Lin has Kade, so it's just me alone." I tell him.

"I know I'm a poor substitute to Lin, but I'm here, Brynn. I'll be here for every storm, just call. I'm not going anywhere."

I nod. "Talk to me about anything," I say.

"Well, my mom refuses to bake me cookies anymore, until I get married and give her grandbabies," he says.

I start laughing. "What?"

"I got home last night, and she had baked cookies for the church. When I tried to eat one, she smacked me with a spatula. She said I don't get cookies, until I give her a daughter-in-law and grandbabies, and in that order, too."

I chuckle. "Well, she can love on Lin's kids. I don't see them waiting too long to have a baby."

"No, I don't either," he says, running a hand through my hair.

It's a move he would have done to make me comfortable all those years ago, and it still works, because I don't remember falling asleep.

* * *

Jasper

I can feel the moment Brynn falls asleep in my arms. It brings a sense of calm over me that she still trusts me and feels safe with me. The storm shows no signs of letting up, so I sit here with her in my arms.

I place a kiss on top of her head, and her scent is still the same, coconut and suntan lotion. When I was in New York, I went on the hunt and found the scent in a candle, which I bought in bulk, and the scent filled my apartment. The few people I had over thought I was nuts, but it smelled like home to me, because Brynn is my home.

Now I know that, and I swear to myself I will never forget again. I should have been there for her on that night. I should have been there to help both of them, and I won't forgive myself for that. If she can find a way to forgive me, I'll forever be grateful and never take her for granted.

I check my watch and see she's been asleep for about an hour, so I gently carry her to her room. Thankfully, her nighttime security guy is in the lobby and helps me with the bedroom door. I lay her on the bed, and that wakes her. She grips the front of my shirt in a panic.

"No, don't leave!" She cries half awake. My heart breaks into pieces right then.

"I'm not going anywhere. I'm going to lock the door, and then, I will get right here in bed with you, okay?"

"Hurry." Is all she says, but she doesn't open her eyes again.

I make quick work of getting ready for bed, and then I stop. I'm still in my kitchen clothes, which I'm sure she doesn't want in her bed. So, I take them off, leaving me in just my boxer briefs. Sighing, I get in bed with her. It's this or her bed smelling like the kitchen for months, so I'm sure she'd agree.

As soon as I'm in bed, she cuddles up to my side, and her hand starts moving over my chest. I wrap one arm around her and take her hand, holding it in mine.

"Go back to sleep, Firefly. I'm not going anywhere."

"I feel safe with you like this, and I'm not scared anymore. It's like how Lin says she feels with Kade." She says.

My throat closes. I want to be that guy for her; to be the one she feels safe with and relies on.

I turn my head to kiss the top of her head, and then she looks up at me. The vulnerability in her eyes is something I rarely see in her, as she leans up and kisses me.

It's a soft kiss, and it's over way too soon. I want her badly, but I won't push her.

"I mean it, Brynn. I'm not going anywhere. Go back to sleep, and I'll be here, when you make up."

"Good." She says, and then throws her leg over mine, attaching herself to my side.

This is what I loved most about snuggling with Brynn. She was all over me, and in a way, it made me feel safe, too.

* * *

Brynn

As I wake up and feel the warm body behind me, I freeze. I crack my eyes and find that I'm in my room. Panic starts to set in, because I don't bring guys to my room. Hell, I don't remember the last time I did anything with a guy. I slowly turn over to find Jasper.

Last night, comes rushing back to me. The storm, sitting in his lap, a brief memory of him bringing me to my room, and saying he isn't going anywhere. I try to get out of bed, but he slings an arm over me and pulls me closer to him.

"Go back to sleep." He mumbles.

"I need to pee," I say.

"Fine, but then, come back to bed." He says, turning over on his back, his gorgeous chest on display. A quick peek under the covers proves he's wearing his boxer briefs and nothing else.

I head to the bathroom, do my business, and then come out and just lean against the door frame, watching him sleep. *In my bed.* He looks like he belongs there, and it feels like he belongs there. Hell, I want him there.

Maybe, it's time to stop fighting so hard to keep some distance and see where this can go. With that thought and a smile on my face, I crawl back into bed, and I wrap myself around his side again.

When I sling my leg over him, his hard cock brushes against my leg, and he groans.

"Sorry," I mumble and start to move my leg away, but he grabs it and pulls it back over his hip.

"Nothing to be sorry for. I want you comfortable." He says and holds me tight, like he thinks I'm going to run away.

Why does the fact that I know he's turned on by me have me so turned on? Is it because he isn't trying to push it any further? I have zero experience with guys that aren't Jasper. I haven't wanted to or even had the time.

My body doesn't seem to care. It's yelling that he's ours, and we need relief. He's so close and warm. Being this near to him is intoxicating. Without thinking, I shift my hips, so I'm straddling him, and I sit up with my hands on his shoulders.

His eyes pop open, and he looks up at me.

"Brynn," he whispers and grabs my hips, but doesn't move me.

I don't break eye contact, as I slowly grind his hard cock against my core, and we both groan.

"Brynn, I haven't even taken you on a date, yet." He says a bit breathlessly.

122

"The wedding was the best date I've ever had. Great food, dancing, friends, and cake." I tell him and grind down again.

"Brynn." He groans, and his smooth muscles flex under me.

"That wasn't a date. Not a proper one. Let me take you on a date, spoil you, and do it up right." He says.

"Okay," I tell him with no hesitation, but I move against his cock again.

"Christ." He groans.

"Don't make me stop." I almost beg.

He looks torn, but finally, he nods.

This time, when I grind, I don't stop, and he uses his grip on my hips to help control the pace. My heart races. He's in his thin boxer briefs, and I'm in my clothes from the night before, but the shorts are short enough, so with a little maneuvering, his cock is rubbing along my lace panties. There's barely anything separating us, and at this moment, if I thought I could get him to agree, I'd try for more, but I don't want to risk him stopping.

The tightening of my muscles starts, and my body floods with heat. I swear, the bulge between my thighs grows, as he grinds his teeth together, watching me. His ab muscles flexing beneath my hands.

"God, you're beautiful." He whispers, as his eyes run all over my body and land, where I'm straddling him.

He moves his hips up and pushes into me harder, causing me to gasp. He keeps one hand firmly on my hips and brings the other to stroke me over my shorts. As he presses down on my clit, I cry out and fall forward, burying my face into his neck.

"Cum for me, Firefly." He whispers in my ear and presses down hard on my clit. The friction is all I need to fall over the edge. I turn my head into his neck and bite down to keep from screaming out. He takes over and grinds against me, prolonging my orgasm. He groans, before wrapping his arms around me.

"I forgot how loud you are." He chuckles a minute later.

"Mmm, we aren't leaving this bed. I can't feel my legs." I tell him.

I don't remember feeling this relaxed in a long time.

"We have a few more hours. Let me hold you." He says.

I don't think a category five hurricane could even get me to move right now.

Chapter 18

Jasper

Why is it when my life starts going well, the universe says too bad? Why can't I just be happy? What did I do to piss it off? I'm beginning to think the universe is on Brynn's side and is going to make me pay for what I did to her nice and slowly.

Today, started off by having Brynn in my arms, and it was better than I dreamed of all those years in New York. But watching her cum? That was life changing, and I know there's no walking away now. This girl has owned my heart from the start, and I don't think I'm ever getting it back.

She seemed to have dropped her walls, after last night. I need to remember to send Kade a huge thank you. I'm not sure what to get him. A fruit basket doesn't seem good enough. Do they make whiskey baskets? Maybe, I will cook him and Lin a special meal. He did say he was missing that Italian family restaurant down the road from his place in Hollywood. I need to ask Lin about it.

I smile and touch my neck. I have to wear my chef's coat buttoned all the way up today, because she did a number on my neck, but I love it. It's her mark on me, and I never thought it would turn me on, as much as it does. Just touching it, has me getting hard again.

She left a few marks on me growing up, and it wasn't as easy to hide. I got a lecture from my mom a few times, but my dad would just smile. He said once that Mom left a few on him. It's like Brynn is marking me as hers. The only thing better would be her ring on my finger, and mine on her hand.

Brynn has been in and out of the kitchen all morning for this or that. I made sure she ate breakfast and a lunch that I made especially for her. The smile I got for those makes me want to do it again and again.

"Jasper, boy. You better get to the lobby. There's trouble." Ken says, as he breaks me from my thoughts. But the look on his face, tells me this isn't time for games. I drop everything, wipe my hands on a towel, and run out to the lobby.

What I find makes my heart sink, but what I hear? Fills me with rage. Why today of all days? I mean, it's the day I finally got Brynn to let her guard down.

Standing in the lobby is Sherri. She was the hostess and event planner at the restaurant I worked at in New York City, and she's talking to Brynn.

Brynn must have just got there, because she smiles at her. "Can I help you?" She asks.

I should speak, but the words don't seem to come out, and I can't reach them fast enough. It's like everything happens in slow motion, and my brain can't decide what to do, so it does nothing, which is worse than anything.

"Oh, I'm looking for my boyfriend, Jasper. I was told he's the chef here." Sherri says.

Brynn's eyes go wide, and I swear I can see each and every brick of those walls, snapping back into place. She pastes on her fake smile that I hate so much. Fuck, it's going to be like last night never happened or worse.

"He is, and I will…"

"What the hell are you doing here, Sherri?" I ask, as I reach them.

Brynn tries to turn and make a run for it, but I wrap an arm around her waist and hold her to me. We need to talk, but I want Sherri out of here now.

"Jasper!" She goes to hug me, and I quickly move behind Brynn, which earns me a dirty look from Sherri, and I'm sure one from Brynn that I can't see. I don't know how to make it any clearer to this girl I don't want her here without making her cry, and that's something my momma would come down here and beat me for in front of the whole town.

"I'm not your boyfriend and never was, so I'm not sure why you're here spreading lies, or even here at all," I say my voice cold.

I don't want any question in Brynn's mind. This girl means nothing to me. Despite what Sherri said, we were never together.

"I miss you. We all thought you'd be back home by now. It can't take this long to help your mom get settled." She says and flips her long, blonde hair over her shoulder.

Her bleached blonde from a bottle hair. Everything about this girl is fake. Her hair, her nails, her lips, her boobs, and her tan, all fake. She's the exact opposite of Brynn, which is what I needed, when I was trying to forget her. The day my heart was breaking, and I needed to forget everything Brynn.

"No, I told you all that I was *moving* here. I packed up and moved. I'm not coming back. I gave up my lease. This is my home, always has been and always will be. It just took me a

127

bit of time to understand that." I bite out.

Brynn starts to squirm, trying to get out of my hold.

"Stop it, Firefly," I say in a soft voice.

"Don't call me that. Let me go, so you and your *girlfriend* can talk." Brynn says.

"Not my girlfriend and never was. You have been the only girl to ever hold that title." I tell her in hopes of showing her what she means to me, but this only seems to piss off Sherri more.

"We were together!" Sherri says.

"No, it was sex. I made that very clear multiple times. I don't want you, so I'm sorry you wasted your time." I tell her.

"I felt it, it was more," Sherri says and places her hand on my arm, giving me what I'm sure is an overly practiced pout.

Her touch makes my skin crawl. Now that I have had the sweetness that is Brynn back in my life, and I have her here in my arms, the touch of this other woman from a dark point in my life, makes me feel dirty.

"It didn't feel like more to me," I tell her, trying to get her hand off my arm.

Of course, this is when Brynn breaks free and makes a run for it. *Damnit.*

"I'm coming for you, Brynn. You can't run far," I call after her.

She doesn't even look back, as she just flips me off and runs, which I'm assuming is right to Lin.

I want to go after her, but I need to make things clear to Sherri and get her out of here. Turning back to her, I level her with a glare. I tried to be nice, but she just sent Brynn running, and no one hurts my girl like that. I'm done being nice. Momma forgive me.

"That girl you just sent running, she's been it for me, since we were kids. I've been in love with her my whole life. I screwed up, when I moved to New York City. You were a distraction and served your purpose. Now, I'm home, and I have another chance with her, and I won't be going back to the city or to you. I can't believe you think I'd be with someone who would hurt a girl like that. I couldn't have made it any more obvious what she meant to me just now. Even if I never win her back, I could never be with the likes of you."

Shock crosses Sherri's face and finally understanding. At least, she has enough self-respect to know when she should cut her losses.

"I'm sorry I bothered you, but you don't have to be an asshole." She says, as she composes herself and slips her sunglasses back on, turning and walking out of the door.

I watch her go, making sure she leaves, and then I run a hand down my face. What a fucking mess. When I turn around, Rich is standing at the desk, not even hiding that he saw everything.

I know this will be all over The Inn by the end of the day, and I hope it will. I want people to help Brynn see that this girl was nothing to me.

"Fuck, that was better than a daytime soap opera." He says, shaking his head.

"Yeah, and I just got Brynn to drop her walls last fucking night. Now, I'm back to square one." I sigh.

"Well, you know she ran straight to Lin. My advice is to go after her, and fix it now. The longer you let it stew, the higher her walls will get again. You know, the more time she has to think up every possible scenario, the harder it will be to talk her down."

I'm not sure if I need to go after her now or give her time, and I'm about to call my mom and ask, when my phone goes off.

Kade: What the fuck happened?

Me: A ghost from my past showed up at the worst fucking time.

Kade: I know things aren't always what they seem, but Brynn says she's your girlfriend.

Me: No, and she never was. That's the term Sherri used, when she asked Brynn to get me.

Kade: Is she gone?

Me: Yes, and I wasn't too nice either. My mom is going to have my hide.

I watch the three bubbles pop up and disappear several times, like he can't decide what to say, before a text finally comes through.

Kade: Sunrise. Back porch.

Fuck, I owe Kade more than he will ever know.

Chapter 19

Brynn

Girlfriend.

That word seems to bounce over and over in my head. Who knew one word could shatter your heart so completely? This is what I get for letting my walls down.

Stupid. Stupid. Stupid.

I won't be doing that. Thankfully, Lin and Kade are easy to find in the lobby of the Sunrise Inn, and I guess, they can tell something is wrong by the look on my face.

"Talk now," I say, heading right back to the small porch between Lin's room and the main back porch. It's private enough we won't be bothered, and most guests don't even know it's here.

I sit down and bring my legs up in front of my chest, wrapping my arms around them. I rest my chin on my knees and let them get settled.

"Spill it," Lin says.

"Jasper has a girlfriend," I tell them.

"Yeah, you," Kade says, giving me an *'aren't you a little slow'* look.

I shake my head. "No, one from New York named *Sherri*."

"What?" They both say, so I tell them about finding the beautiful blonde in the lobby, and her asking for her boyfriend, Jasper. Ending with, Jasper's reaction, and finally, breaking free to come here.

Lin and Kade look at each other. I don't even know what to say about all this. They seem to have a silent conversation. Married barely a week, and they have already mastered that.

"So, first off, you know as well as we do that girl isn't his girlfriend. She sounds just like the girls who tried to use me for their fifteen minutes of fame, or the gold diggers that were always around." Kade says.

"How would Jasper give her fifteen minutes of fame? And he doesn't have any money worthy of a gold digger." I tell him.

"No, but his family has a decent net worth, and she could have looked into him and saw an opportunity. The net worth of those restaurants has skyrocketed, since his dad opened them. With their location right on the water, I bet the property alone is worth a million each, easily." Lin points out.

I just shake my head, trying to sort it all out. I know she's right. Hell, the net worth on these Inns is pretty large, but that doesn't mean we have the cash to back it up. I guess, it wouldn't stop people from wanting their share. Add that to the reasons why it's so hard to date.

"Did she leave?" Lin asks.

"I don't know. I left them to talk the moment I could break from Jasper's hold. I couldn't take sitting there, watching the lovers' fight going on."

Kade is on his phone and looks angry. Part of me is hoping he's giving Jasper a piece of his mind.

"You opened up, huh?" Lin says, watching me.

"Yeah, he took care of me last night. He didn't leave my side, and I saw my Jasper. The one who always took care of me and put me first. I told him about why the storms upset me, and even talked about that day." I say, swallowing the lump in my throat. "I thought it meant something, but stupid me."

"It did mean something. It meant everything." Jasper says.

I look up and find him standing on the beach on the other side of the porch rail.

"That woman is a master manipulator. I quickly found out that almost everyone in my inner circle was. They all want to rise to the top through any means necessary, and they don't care who they hurt along the way. I hated that life." He says, making his way up the porch and sitting down beside me.

"Can I talk to her?" Jasper asks Lin and Kade.

"No," I tell him and try to stand, but he uses this to pull me into his lap.

Lin and Kade exchange another look. "Yes, but I expect a full report." Lin says to me, as they stand up.

"Traitors," I say, but they just smile.

Kade wraps an arm around Lin's waist and guides her back inside.

"I tried to date in New York. I thought I could just move on, and everything would be fine. Only I couldn't. Every date reminded me of you. She would dress like you, order the same thing off the menu you would, or she'd say something you would, and instantly, I wanted you there. Then, the rest of the date I was comparing them to you. You would have done this, and you wouldn't have done that."

He stops and seems to stare off into the distance, and then, his arms tighten around me.

"Not one girl made me feel the way you did." His eyes shoot

to mine, and he reaches up, tucking some hair behind my ear. "Like you still do."

His hand lightly traces down my cheek to my chin, and he runs his thumb over my bottom lip.

He sighs and drops his hand, as he wraps it back around me.

"Then, I just wanted to find a way to dull the pain of losing you. I wanted to forget; not that I could. So, that's when Sherri entered the picture. It was just sex, and she knew that from the start."

My whole body stiffens, and suddenly, I'm too close to Jasper. He was with that girl. She's so much prettier than me, and she's everything I'm not.

"Brynn, don't let your mind run off. I shut down and became this emotionless jerk. I didn't care about her, her needs, or anything. We didn't talk; it was just sex and go. But every time? Every time in my head, I was with you. My favorite memory was prom night, and a close second was the weekend we spent in Wilmington right before I left. Those memories are what got me by. Then, Dad died, and I stopped it all. I haven't been with her, since before he died. I shut everyone out."

My head is telling me to be pissed and run, but in my heart, I'm reaching for him, because all these years, I was always with him, too. In my darkest hours, I'd reach for my favorite memories of us, and it would pull me through. I get it. Not that I will admit that to him, even now.

"Then, my mom called. She said needed me here, and the businesses needed me. But I realized, that I needed you. Even if you kept me at arm's length, just being able to see and talk to you, is what I needed. The day you threw the kiwi at me was one of the best days of my life, Firefly."

I try not to smile, but the memory of the first time he called me that, fills my head. It was the summer I was fourteen, and we had just gotten out of school. Lin, Jasper, Travis, and I were hanging out at The Sunrise, and we had heard of the rare synchronous fireflies up in Tennessee. We talked about them for weeks, and finally, mine and Lin's parents packed the four of us up one night, and they took us to see them.

We were so excited to have Jasper and Travis with us, and I remember being mesmerized. How the fireflies would all light at the same time and seemed to do a dance. We learned they flash for mating, and I turned to Jasper and said, *"It's the most beautiful way to say I love you."* I had tears in my eyes.

"It is, isn't it?" He said, wiping the tears. He kissed me right there in the middle of the dancing fireflies. *Our first kiss.* And the nickname, has followed me ever since.

Our first kiss wasn't like a normal first kiss. I swear, our entire future ahead of us was in that kiss. I didn't see this rocky path, but one thing Mom and Dad always said, is that in any relationship there's good and bad, and you have to stick around and work through it to get to the good.

"I want no one but you, Firefly. From that first kiss, it's always been you." He whispers the same thoughts I was just having.

He moves ever so slowly, until his lips dance across mine, like he's too scared to push me. So instead, I pull him to me, as I wrap my arms around his neck and deepen the kiss. The moment I do his entire body relaxes, and his hands move up and down my back, to my hair, and down to my waist, like he can't decide where to hold me.

"Don't block me out, Brynn. Let me in, and let me show you how great we can be together." He says, kissing that sensitive area on my neck.

I couldn't form a complete sentence if I tried. All I can do is feel. Feel his warm breath on my neck. Feel his hands on me. Feel how hard he is for me.

That last one has me turning and straddling his lap. He pulls back just enough to look up at me, as hope fills his eyes. I take his face in my hands and kiss him, showing him with my actions what he means to me.

I'm desperate to get back the feeling we had this morning, the connection, and the peace. But as soon as I grind down on him, he stops me.

"Not here, Firefly, and not where anyone can see you." He says.

"Let's go back to my room," I suggest.

He looks at me, studying my face, and for what, I'm not sure.

"Tell me you're mine, and that you will give us a chance. Tell me you know I'm yours, and we can go to your room and get the relief you need." He says.

I want him, but I need time to process it, too.

I sigh. "Make you a deal. We leave the day after tomorrow to go to the state capital and present our case on the Main Street issue. Come with us, and let's take some time to be us, outside of this town. Then, when we get back, we can really talk, okay?"

"Yes, I'll be there. But Brynn?" He raises one hand to the side of my face, and I can't help but lean into him.

"Yeah?"

"You can take all the time you need. I want you to be sure, because I'm not going anywhere. Not ever again, okay?"

All I can do is nod. What do you say to that? Thank you seems woefully inadequate, so I just lean down and softly kiss him.

Chapter 20

Jasper

One thing about having an ex Hollywood movie star for a friend is that he likes to spoil us. Kade wanted the girls to relax on the drive into Raleigh. It's a two to three hour drive, depending on traffic, so Kade rented a car with a driver for the trip. We're also staying in a two-bedroom suite at one of the hotels near where the meeting is.

When I tried to pay him for mine and Brynn's half, he refused. He just made me promise to take this time to win her over. So, that's what I plan to do.

Right now, the girls are discussing their plans for the meeting and going over their talking points for later this afternoon. Brynn is sitting next to me, and she's curled into my side the way Lin is curled into Kade's side.

She's letting me in, and I'm not going to take it for granted. We're sharing a room in the suite, and I can't wait to hold Brynn in my arms all night.

The time seems to fly, and before we know it, we're checking into our hotel. The moment we walk into the suite, the girls burst into giggles and have to check out everything in the small kitchen, the living area, and both bedrooms. They are talking business, what ideas they could steal, and what's the practicality of this or that, but the whole time their faces are lit up.

"Thanks again for this," I tell Kade, as we stand by the door, watching them.

"I'd do anything to put that smile on Lin's face." He says.

"Yeah, I'd do the same for Brynn," I tell him.

He looks over at me. "Good. Make it happen more often, because the more Brynn smiles, the more Lin smiles."

"I'm doing my best, and I appreciate all your help." I tell him.

He shrugs. "I'd do anything for Brynn, because she's always done everything for Lin. Just don't fuck it up."

"Easier said than done," I tell him.

"Don't I know it," Kade says, his eyes back on Lin.

The girls get dressed and ready for their presentation, and then, we're back in the car and on our way. Looking at Brynn, you might not know she's nervous, but her giveaway is that she's twirling her hair.

"You're going to do amazing, Firefly," I whisper into her ear.

Her eyes meet mine. "I hope so. The town is depending on us doing well today."

"This isn't on you. If this doesn't work, we go another route. We're in this together the four of us, okay?" I tell her.

This seems to calm her, because she drops her hair and rests her head on my shoulder.

When we get there, it's a flurry of activities. We're whisked into some large meeting room. Kade and I are given seats in the back, and the girls are taken to the front of the room behind a podium.

They deliver their cases flawlessly with the stats on tourism now, and the history they dug up on Main Street. They present what they could do with the museum and the national landmark seal. They have plans on advertising it, and how it would increase tourism to not just Hummingbird Island, but to the state. How they can link it to other historic sites like Bath, North Carolina. Then, they show the plans of what the mayor is trying to do now, the history of the land developer, how it will destroy the buildings, and the history. They even have plans to build a replica lighthouse where the old one stood.

They have everything prepared with photos, graphs, and more. I'm so proud of how well they presented their case, and I'm not the only one.

"Wow, they did great," Kade whispers next to me.

"Yeah, they did." I agree.

They take some questions, and then a recess is called for the committee to go over everything, and we are told to come back tomorrow morning.

"Okay, we're taking you girls out to dinner to celebrate." Kade says, once we're back in the car.

"We don't even know if we won," Lin says.

"It doesn't matter, because your presentation was excellent, and it looks like it will go your way. Either way, you did it, and we're celebrating." Kade replies.

"I agree. You were both amazing up there. You had me convinced." I tell them.

"You were already convinced, so your opinion is irrelevant." Brynn waves me off.

Noticing Kade and Lin, whispering to each other, I lean down to Brynn's ear.

"Watching you up there, commanding that room, it made

me hot. Trust me, you had them convinced." I whisper.

Her cheeks flush, and fuck, my cock gets hard at the sight. Thankfully, we pull up to our hotel.

"We're going to check on things at The Inn and get ready," Lin says.

"Meet back out here at six?" Kade asks.

"Sounds good." I agree, as Lin and Kade head to their room, and I follow Brynn to ours.

"I guess, I should check in at Sunset, too," Brynn says, as she sits down on the edge of the bed.

"Go ahead," I tell her.

I sit against the headboard and pull her to sit between my legs with her back to my chest. As she talks to Rich, she rests her head against my shoulder.

"You found what in the pool?" Brynn asks.

"Oh my. Put it in my office, and then hang a sign up at the front desk. No picture, but make sure whoever comes asking for it, can describe it perfectly." She says.

"Okay, let me know," Brynn says, before hanging up.

"What happened?" I ask.

"Oh, some kid turned in a woman's wedding ring set. Rich says the rock is huge, and it looks to be real. So hopefully, we find the owner." She says.

"And if you don't?"

"Well, I'll hold it in the safe tagged with the date found. I have some in there that I have held for over two years. I hate to get rid of them just in case." She sighs.

"You need a nap. I'm sure the presentation matched with the early morning took a lot out of you." I tell her.

"A nap sounds heavenly. Snuggle with me?" She asks.

Like I would say no to that. Time spent with this girl in my arms, I'd lie there all day.

"Of course. Lay down." I tell her.

She gets comfortable, and I lay behind her, spooning and holding her close. She's asleep in no time at all. Making sure I have an alarm set, I'm not far behind her.

* * *

Dinner was delicious. Of course, Kade spared no expense, taking the girls to a nice place and making sure they ordered what they wanted and dessert, too. As soon as we got back to the hotel, Lin and Kade went back to their room, and we went to ours.

"I don't remember the last time I ate so much," Brynn says, as she lies down on the bed.

"Eat too much?" I chuckle.

"Way too much. It was so good, and I didn't want to stop." She groans.

"Why don't you take a nice hot bath and relax a bit?" I tell her.

The bathroom here is every girls dream. The bathtub is a large claw-foot tub that can easily fit two people.

"That sounds wonderful. Maybe, you should join me." She rolls her head to look at me and offers a small smile, before getting off the bed and walking into the bathroom, leaving the door open just a crack.

This is such a bad idea. We're supposed to be taking it slow. She hasn't even agreed to be mine, but I want to get in that tub with her so bad. The thought of a naked Brynn, rubbing up against me, is almost too much. Yet, leaving her in there wanting me is something I can't do. Though, I can give her a happy medium.

As I enter the bathroom, I find her already in the tub with her hair pulled up on top of her head. She looks over and smiles at me.

"Decided to join me?" She asks.

I roll up the sleeves on my long sleeve button-up shirt and kneel down next to the tub, as I grab the washcloth and her soap.

Brynn watches my every move, but she doesn't say anything. The bubbles she added to the water rest just at the top of her breasts, hiding most of her body from me.

"Lean forward, Firefly," I whisper, and she does, leaning her chest against her bent legs. She rests her arms on her knees and her head on her arms, as she watches me.

I take my time and wash her back, the length of her neck, and her shoulders all while keeping eye contact with her.

"Lean back," I whisper, and she does.

Keeping my eyes on her, I start at her shoulders, wash across her chest, before washing one breast, and then the other. Her breathing picks up, and her lips part, but she still holds my gaze.

I move down and swirl over her stomach, before going down one hip and washing one leg and foot. I bring the washcloth back up the inside of her leg and lightly across her mound, causing her to whimper. Then, I wash the other leg and foot the same way.

This time, when I reach her pussy, I drop the washcloth and brush over her with my fingers. Gasping, she breaks eye contact, throwing her head back against the tub. With a moan, her legs open wider for me.

I lightly stroke her clit and watch the stiff peaks of her nipples poke above the waterline, as her chest heaves. I remember Brynn's body, like it was yesterday. She's still just as sensitive, and when I insert a finger into her pussy, I swear she's tighter than I remember. I stroke her pussy from the inside, as I continue to strum her clit.

Her walls start to flutter around my finger, so I add a second finger.

"Jasper!" She gasps.

"You're so gorgeous," I tell her honestly.

Her eyes meet mine again, and I'm lost. I give her clit a little more pressure, and her legs start to shake. She grips the side of the tub, as her knuckles turn white, and her back arches.

I move my other hand over her mouth just in time to stifle her screaming my name, as she cums.

"I've never seen anything so beautiful," I tell her, when she opens her eyes again. Wanting more, I run my hand lightly up her stomach to her breasts, and then rub my thumb over each nipple, before moving up and cupping her face. Then, I pull her in for a kiss.

Her tongue wars with mine for dominance, and I smile against her lips.

"Slow down, Firefly. We have all night," I whisper.

"I want you so bad." She says and tries to pull me into the tub with her.

"Not tonight, Firefly. Not until you're mine." I pull back, looking into her eyes. I need her to know this is real, this is what I want, and this is everything.

She sighs. "You'll still snuggle with me, right?"

"Of course, I don't think I can sleep without you in my arms now. I've become addicted." I tell her.

She smiles, looking down at my cock, which is rock hard and tenting my pants. There's no hiding it.

"What about you?" She asks.

I smirk. "Don't worry about me. I've gotten good at taking care of myself," I tell her.

When the blush on her cheeks deepens, I just laugh.

"Get dressed. You need your rest." I say.

My fist and I have a cold shower date tonight, but it's completely worth it.

Chapter 21

Brynn

It's been a few days, since we went to Raleigh for the meeting to save Main Street. The next morning, we went back to see what they had decided and were shocked they agreed to move forward in preserving our Main Street. I think we were still surprised all the way home.

The next battle we have is getting the permits for the villas. We're waiting for the news to hit the mayor. The state is going to be delivering a nice formal notice to him any day now.

No matter how excited I am we won, when I remember that day, all I think about is that night in the bathtub with Jasper. I wanted so much more, but Jasper not letting it go further, was the right decision. I've been toying with if I can be his, and if so, how much of my heart do I have to give away?

I put those thoughts away, as I get ready for one of the first Sunset events on the beach that someday will become The Chasing the Sun Villas. I have people setting up a drink station and bringing out blankets to sit on.

Just as I'm about to go over and check it out myself, Jasper steps out of the kitchen.

"Hey, Firefly. Ready to head over?" He asks.

This event is all I have been able to talk about. Being able to have it on the beach this season, is what everyone has been wanting. The views from The Sunset roof are beautiful, but it's just not the same, as sitting on the beach and watching the sun disappear into the water.

To finally have it right on the beach, is why it's the only thing I've talked about the last few days, as I made preparations and tried to get ready.

"I am. You're coming with me?" I ask him.

"Nothing could keep me away." He smiles.

He takes my hand in his, and we walk across the street to the west side of our little point of The Island and see some guests have already shown up. He gives my hand a squeeze, and we go mingle and check to make sure everyone is set and comfortable.

One couple on the far side of the beach has a camera and a tripod set up. There's another family with some young kids, chasing each other at the water's edge, and a few couples snuggled up on blankets we scattered around. Rich and Ken are here together, checking on everyone and helping set up.

"I can't believe this is actually happening!" Lin says, as she runs up to hug me.

I hold her tight. "Me either. Both of our parents would be so excited," I say.

Kade walks up and puts an arm around Lin, then and pulls me in for a side hug. Her smile matches mine. It's so big that it lights up her whole face, and when Kade looks at her, he supports a matching one.

"Thank you for this, Kade," I say, looking out over the beach again.

"Nah, this is all you." He waves me off.

"Grab a blanket; get comfy," I tell them, and then watch them head off and find their own little spot on the beach.

"Let's find a place, too," Jasper says, and I turn to find him with a blanket over his arm. I let him lead us to a spot just far enough away from everyone, but still close enough, if they need us.

He spreads the blanket out on the sand, and then sits down, before pulling me to sit between his legs, my back to his chest. He wraps his arms around me, resting his elbows on his knees, and his chin on my shoulder, as we both watch the sky start turning a beautiful orange with a hint of red.

It reminds me of many evenings we had like this growing up. We'd watch the sunset at The Cove. The Cove is a local's only beach, because it's behind some private homes. There's a path between two homes that only the locals know about. In the summer, when the beaches are overtaken by tourists, it's great to have a place to get away from them.

"I hope you have been thinking, Brynn, because I meant what I said. I want a second chance." He whispers in my ear.

Why do those words send butterflies swarming in my stomach? They want me to take the leap and not care that there's no safety net to catch me. But my brain kicks in, saying this isn't a good idea. I can't afford to be left heartbroken again and trying to pick up the pieces at this point in my life. We're starting this new adventure with the villas, which requires my time and energy.

"I will wait as long as you need, Brynn. I'm here for the long haul." He says, almost like he can read my mind.

I get the feeling he doesn't just mean here on The Island. I think he means in my life, in my kitchen, in my Inn, and in my space. The more I think about it, the more I can live with the decision to let him in.

I can't imagine The Inn without him now, and I don't want, too. The kitchen has never run better, and the staff is happier.

I twist sideways to gaze into his eyes. The look he gives me back is the one Kade gives Lin all the time. The one I keep saying I want. Right then, my heart overrules my brain, and I decide to give him an opening, though a guarded one. Another chance, the last one, because in order to move forward, I need to know.

Can we make it together? How can I move on with someone else with the 'what if' from Jasper, hanging over my head? It wouldn't be fair to me or the next guy. Not that I want there to be a next guy because that means there will be a next girl and I don't think I can handle watching that.

"Okay," I tell him.

His face breaks out into a smile.

"Okay, yes?" He asks to be sure.

"Yes, one more chance." I tell him.

"You won't regret it." He says and leans forward to give me a light kiss.

Thankfully, he doesn't push the kiss out here in front of everyone.

"You're missing the sunset." He says, when I don't open my eyes right away.

I turn just as the sun is starting to dip into the water.

Everyone stills, even the kids, and watches, as the sun disappears. It's so quiet, like all of Hummingbird Island is pausing.

The moment the last of the sun dips below the water, people start moving, and The Island comes back to life.

149

Kade lights up the bonfire, and everyone gathers around. This is definitely better than the events on the roof.

Chapter 22

Jasper

I still can't believe Brynn agreed to give me another chance. I've been floating all day, and I think I'm freaking out the kitchen staff with how much I've been smiling. It's been a slow day in the kitchen, so I head out to decide on dinner for Brynn and me.

I've spent a good part of the afternoon planning it. She's wrapping up her second Sunset event of the season, when I meet up with her in the lobby. I'm no longer wearing my kitchen clothes, as I have changed into my good pants and a button-up shirt. Brynn dressed up for the event at my request and is in a tan, lace dress with a brown, leather belt around her waist and matching brown, cowboy boots.

She left her hair down, and I wonder if she did that, because she remembered how much I love her hair that way. I want to think she did.

I hold out my hand for her, and she walks right to me, taking it without hesitation. I pull her hand up and twirl her around.

"You look stunning," I tell her.

"You look pretty handsome there yourself. Big plans?" She

asks.

"Yep, got me a hot date," I say and tuck her hand into the crook of her arm.

"Oh, really?" She raises an eyebrow at me, and I just smile at her.

"Yep." I say, as I lead us to her room.

"You have a plan to get laid?" She cocks her head to the side.

"No, that's not proper first date manners. Just open the door." I tell her.

I had Lin's help here. Her porch is lit up with as many candles as I could fit. They surround the table, which has our dinner on it covered and waiting for us.

"Jasper!" She gasps. "What did you do?"

"Well, I knew the chance of getting you away from The Inn for an evening during the season was slim to none, so this is the second best option. Will you have dinner with me?" I ask her.

"Of course." She says, and then shocks me, when she leans up and kisses my cheek, before taking a seat at the table.

I recover just in time to help pull out her chair, before sitting across from her.

"So, what's for dinner?" She asks.

I smile. "Open up and see," I tell her.

"Mac and cheese?" She asks, when she takes the lid off.

"Not any mac and cheese." I smile, as she digs in.

"Oh my, gosh, lobster mac and cheese. You remembered?" She asks shocked.

On our first date, I took her to my family restaurant. She had been talking about this lobster mac and cheese she saw on some food TV show. So, my dad and I worked on a few recipes, using my mom as a taste tester, until we found the perfect one, and that's what we had on our first date.

"Of course, I remember. There isn't a minute of our time together that I've forgotten. There may be a few I wanted to forget, but I remember them all." I say, as I hold her gaze.

She stares for a moment, before clearing her throat and digging into her dinner.

After the first bite, she groans. "This is even better than the last time I had it." She says.

"Well, I have picked up a few new tricks since then." I wink at her.

Dinner flows great. We talk about our time apart, and the happy stuff we did. Funny gossip about the people in town, and suggestions she has gotten on The Sunset event.

Once she finishes eating, I pull out my phone and put on some music. I stand and hold my hand out to her.

"Dance with me?" I ask her.

Her smile lights up her pretty face, as she stands and takes my hand. I pull her off the porch into the sand, and we dance.

"Last time I danced, before Lin's wedding, was at prom with you." She says.

"I remember at prom I spent every dance, trying to hide how hard you made me just being so close. You were so beautiful in that emerald, green dress." I tell her.

"I still have it. Couldn't bear to get rid of it." She smiles and rests her head on my shoulder.

"Well, keep it. The memory of what we did after prom is one of my favorites." I chuckle.

That night wasn't the first time we had sex, but it was the first time we made love.

"It was one of the best nights of my life," I tell her.

"I agree it was." She sighs.

I pull her closer, not hiding how she makes me feel. I'm hard as steel, and having her so near, is intoxicating. Her scent fills my lungs, and her skin on mine makes my body crave her.

But not on a first date. I won't mess this up.

"Can we go for a walk on the beach?" She asks.

"Of course," I tell her and grab my phone. I shoot off a quick text for one of the kitchen guys to come out and clean up the porch. Then, I take her hand, and we walk down the two shorelines.

Brynn switches sides to put me between the water and her, and something Kade said to me in passing about Lin comes to mind.

"Brynn, have you been back in the water since?" I ask her.

She hesitates for a minute. "No, and not even on a boat. I hate even driving over the bridge." She says honestly.

I get that. Her parents died in the ocean right off The Island, and it was the same storm that caused the one bridge in and out of town to collapse.

Maybe, this time, when the storm knocked out the bridge, it was a good thing, because it trapped Kade on The Island and brought him and Lin together. It also pushed Brynn and me together.

"Ever think the bridge going out this time was your parents way of pushing you and Lin to your happily ever after? Think your parents got tired of you waiting around?" I ask.

She's quiet for so long that I think maybe she didn't hear me.

"I thought so for Lin. The events were just too perfect. It's like maybe her mom handpicked Kade and delivered him on a silver platter. The jury is still out on you." She forces a smile, but I see the thought in her eyes.

"Every so often something happens, and I look back and

154

just know my dad had a hand in it. I'm pretty sure my dad was conspiring with your parents to trap us together like this. Not long after the bridge went out, I felt this pull to go visit my dad's grave. Lin and Kade showed up. She came over and offered me an olive branch that I didn't know I needed. Helped me heal in a way. If I didn't have the pull, I wouldn't have been there." I tell her.

"Well, our parents always did like to meddle and play matchmaker." She says.

"Very true." By this time, we have walked around The Island point and are over on the other side, where we held The Sunset event.

"How long before it stops hurting so much?" I ask her.

She seems to know exactly what I mean. "I don't know if the pain of losing them really stops, or we just become used to it. I think around two years I got so busy I forgot to grieve. By the time things slowed down, it hurt a whole lot less." She says.

We turn and start heading back to The Inn, and once again, she changes sides to keep me between her and the water. I take that moment to wrap my arm around her, as if to say, I won't let anything take her away from me.

"I hope you know you can talk to me about this. I've been there, so has Lin. Either one of us would be happy to listen." She says.

"I know, Firefly, I know," I say and desperately search for a way to get our date back on track.

"So, think you can sneak away from The Inn tomorrow mid-day?" I ask her. I want to get our next date lined up.

"Rich is working, so I think I can do that." She says with a smile.

"Good, I'm going to take you on one of my favorite dates we used to do, when we were still in school."

"What's that?" She asks.

"You'll see." I smile.

"Well, at least tell me what to wear." She says.

"What you normally wear will be perfect," I say.

She chuckles, as we make our way into the lobby. I walk her to her door, and she stops and turns around.

"You coming in?" She asks.

I lean down and kiss her. A sweet, soft kiss with a promise of more to come.

"No, I'm not. That's not proper first date behavior." I smirk.

"But." She starts, and I cut her off with another kiss.

"Good night, Firefly. See you tomorrow for date number two." I tell her, turning and walking away.

Walking away, is the hardest thing I have had to do in a long time. Am I crazy for walking away from the perfect girl who wants me her bed? I want to be there so bad it hurts. I want to hold her and wake up to see her in the morning, when her walls are down, and she's a little shy.

When I get home, I find mom reading on the couch, like I do every night.

"What has you smiling like the cat that just caught the canary?" She asks, as she sets down her book.

"I just had a date with Brynn. An amazing date at that." I tell her but make no move to go sit down. "I'm going to bed, so if you want details, you'll have to make me breakfast, and something with bacon," I call over my shoulder.

My mom makes the best omelets, and while she cooks breakfast for us most mornings, I know she will go over the top for the gossip tomorrow. That makes me smile, as I head

156

right to the bathroom to take a shower.

As I step under the ice, cold water, it doesn't stop my thoughts. Mostly, flashes of Brynn in that green prom dress. But the Brynn I know now has more curves, a sassy smile, and looks like a goddess, when she cums.

Fuck. Knowing what she looks like, when she cums has been hell. It's all I can think about, because I want to make her do it again and again. But now that we're dating, I won't rush this. I will wait for at least the third date rule. My dick doesn't agree though, as he's hard and angry with me.

I give my balls a tug, trying to relive the pressure, but it just makes thoughts of Brynn's mouth around my cock flash through my mind. Punching a fist to the wall, I brutally grab my cock and start stroking him. I picture Brynn in the bathtub at the hotel, only this time, I get in with her.

When I get in, she turns and climbs on top of me and sinks down on my dick. With her warmth engulfing me, and her perfect tits eye level with the water, and the bubbles cascading down, she wraps her arms around me and starts riding me.

Then, flashes of prom night, her looking into my eyes, while I slipped inside of her, and all the I love you's exchanged that night, when she came on my cock. That memory always does it, and my cum spurts from my cock and right down the drain with the cold water.

I lean against the wall, as the orgasm runs through my body, but it's gone as fast as it came. I'm reminded of how long it's been, since I've been inside my girl and groan.

This is the worst self-induced torture ever.

Chapter 23

Brynn

I'm dressed, and in the lobby, waiting for Jasper and trying to think what our second date could possibly be. I realized last night that I need to schedule some best friend time to get Lin caught up on my dates with Jasper. Well, on everything Jasper related.

We have both been so busy that we now need to schedule our best friend time. We used to meet every night for dinner, no matter how busy were. Add in two guys, and that went out of the window. She and Kade have been in their little love bubble, and I can't remember the last time I saw her so happy, which makes me happy.

"Hey, there, Firefly." Jasper's voice comes from behind me.

I turn and smile, "Am I dressed appropriately? Do you know how hard it is for a girl to dress for a date, when she has no idea where she's going? It just isn't right you…" he cuts me off with a kiss. It's a chaste kiss, but a kiss that knocks my mind blank all the same.

"You're dressed perfectly. Ready to go?" He asks.

"Yep," I smile up at him.

He takes my hand and pulls me towards the sidewalk.

"What?" I ask him, thinking we should be heading to his car.

"We're going to walk. Remember all those times we didn't have a car to use, so we walked everywhere. I loved it, because I got to hold your hand, and we just talked about everything." He says.

He's right. I'd tell him every little detail from school, and he'd talk about every little detail from the restaurants with his dad. It's how we got to know each other.

"Okay, so what are we talking about?"

"Well, I want to know about that first year or so after you took over The Inn. I know we keep avoiding our time apart, and I get it, but it's a big part of your life that I don't know about."

"Where do you want me to start?" I ask.

"Well, my mom filled me in all the days leading up to the funereal, and I was at the funeral, so tell me about the after." He says.

I go on to tell him about meeting with the lawyers and getting all the assets transferred to my name. The conferences with the accountant to figure out the best way to keep The Inn and the house, and where I should live. How it was the accountant's idea I live at The Inn and rent out my parents' house, during the season.

I talk about moving out of the house I grew up in and redecorating it. About moving into The Inn and decorating my room there. About how I struggled to get my footing, and how most of the staff supported me.

How the first guy I fired was Rich's boss, and then promoted Rich in his place. How I had to learn every part of the business I didn't know. The hours spent learning from everyone. All the way to Kade showing up and asking me to help him with his PR this year, because I had taught myself to do it for both Inns.

We have been circling downtown, while we talked, and he stops.

"I don't think I've told you how proud I am of you. You dove in headfirst and took all this on. I should have been there, and I know that. Though, that's another story, but seeing all you have done, takes my breath away." He says, shocking me.

I take a deep breath, "Okay, enough with the heavy for the date. Where are we going?" I ask, changing the subject, and thankfully, he lets me.

"For our favorite treat on a hot summer day like this." He smiles.

"Ice cream?" I ask.

"Yep. Tell me your favorite is still chocolate chip cookie dough?" He asks.

"Of course. Is yours still black cherry?" I ask him.

"Yes, and let me tell you, with how big New York City is, I couldn't find a single place that had ice cream as good as they have here. I don't get it. A huge city, and no one knew how to make ice cream." He shakes his head.

"Last I checked, I'm pretty sure as a chef you have to know how to make ice cream." I tease him.

"Yes, I do, but it's all in the recipe, and I never could replicate it either. I even tried to have my mom bribe the recipe out of the owners, and they wouldn't budge." He pouts.

I just laugh, as we enter and get in line. While we wait, I check out all the local handmade items on the display tables around the store.

Jasper orders our cones, and we head outside to walk the

pier, as we eat them. But when we get to the start of the pier, Jasper stops.

"Is this okay? I know you don't do the water, but what about the pier?" He asks.

"The pier doesn't bother me. It's okay." I assure him.

"Do you remember the lighthouse?" He asks.

At the end of the pier, used to be a lighthouse. It was one of the first structures on The Island, but when I was six, a hurricane came through and destroyed it. The town wasn't thinking of its history and tore the rest of it down, instead of trying to rebuild and preserve it.

"Yeah, I don't think I was ever inside it, though. I hope the state decides to rebuild it, because I think it could be a huge draw." I tell him.

"My dad took me inside once. I don't think we were supposed to be there, but you know him, he always pulled favors. We climbed to the top, and I remember looking out over The Island, thinking what an amazing place I got to live. I knew then I would leave to be a chef in a big city, learn everything I could, and then settle back here to raise a family. The storm came through and hit the lighthouse not long after." He says.

We sit down on one of the benches at the end of the pier and eat our ice cream, while we watch the guys fishing. No matter what time of the day, you can always find someone out here fishing in almost any weather.

"My dad tried to teach me to fish out here once. I wasn't patient enough." I laugh.

"My dad always said he'd rather cook it than catch it. But he loved going out on the water, more for the quiet than to fish." Jasper laughs.

The conversation stays light, as we talk about kids we went to school with, and where they are now.

When we stand to head back to The Inn, I turn to face Main Street and stop to take it in. Pulling out my phone, I snap a picture for The Inn's social media.

"I'm glad all this will be saved. I can't imagine all these buildings being torn down for those ugly stores. There would be no reason to come enjoy the view." I shake my head.

"Well, you and Lin saved it. I'm actually surprised we haven't heard anything from the mayor about it." He says.

"You and me both," I say, as he takes my hand.

He stops me right in the middle of the sidewalk in the middle of downtown.

"Remember this spot?" He asks.

I take a moment and look around. We're in front of his seafood restaurant on the waterside of the road. Then, it hits me.

"This is where you asked me to prom." I smile.

"It is. It's also where I kissed you the second time, and the day you became my girlfriend the first time." He smiles.

I remember that day. I was hanging out with him and his dad, trying out the new desserts they were thinking of featuring. Then, we came out for a walk, and we stood watching the waves, and I was thinking of our kiss just a week earlier.

Then, out of the blue, he asked me to be his girlfriend, and I said yes, and then he kissed me again. He said that was the best perk of me being his girlfriend, being able to kiss me.

I smile and pull him in for a kiss right there in front of everyone with the sea breeze in my hair, and the sun on my face. He wraps his arms around my waist and kisses me back.

"Best perk of being your girlfriend is being able to kiss you anytime I want," I smirk, when I pull back.

His whole face lights up with a smile that spreads across his face.

"I have to agree." He says and pulls me in for another quick kiss, before taking my hand, and we keep walking.

"I love reliving the old memories with you, but I want to make new ones. Lots of new ones that are better than the old ones. I'm not here for a trip down memory lane. I'm here for you." He says.

"I know, but it's nice to remember the good times. We had a lot of them."

"I agree."

We walk the rest of the way back, just enjoying the sun and each other's company.

"Is that the mayor's car?" I ask, pointing to the car parked in the fire lane in front of The Sunrise. A sinking feeling in my gut.

"Yep, guess he was finally notified. Let's go rescue Lin from the mayor's hissy fit." He says.

Chapter 24

Jasper

I follow Brynn into The Sunrise Inn, and the scene in the lobby makes my blood run cold. The mayor isn't just yelling at Lin, like I expected to find. No, he has her pinned to the wall, his hands on her shoulders, and his face an inch from hers. I'm infuriated and want to break his neck.

Where the hell is Kade?

I look at the girl at the front desk, and she can't be more than eighteen or nineteen, and she's cowering away from the situation. I can't blame her. Taking Brynn's hand, I pull her over there.

"Hey, call Kade," I tell the girl at the front desk.

Okay, at least, he's on his way. My mind races with everything. I need to make sure Brynn is safe at the same time, and getting to the mayor without killing him with my bare hands.

"I did, and the cops," she whispers.

"Where is Dale?" I ask about Sunrise's daytime security.

"There was a problem with a couple yelling upstairs." She says, and I nod.

"Video," is all I have to say to Brynn, before she has her phone up to record all this for the cops.

"I suggest you get your hands off her for your own safety." I bellow across the lobby, getting the mayor's attention.

He turns his head, and his eyes land on Brynn. I step in front of her, because the thought of his eyes on her makes my skin crawl. He's always looked at her like some piece of meat, even when she was underage, and it's never set well with me.

He doesn't drop his hands. "Ahhh, there's the other one." He sneers.

The terrified look on Lin's face says enough is enough.

I make my way across the lobby, not hiding that he's my destination, and yet, the asshole doesn't remove his hands from Lin. This guy really is as stupid as he looks.

"I said remove your hands, or I'll do it," I grit out, when I'm just a few steps away from him.

This is also, when Kade bursts through the door. I can tell the moment his eyes land on Lin, and he sees the mayor's hands on her.

"You son of a bitch!" Kade yells. I reach them faster and shove the mayor hard enough to throw him off balance, but not hard enough to throw him against the coffee table, like I want, too.

He regains his balance quickly and tries to take a swing at me. I block it, grabbing his arm and swinging him around. Then, I put my hands around his throat and slam him hard up against the wall he had Lin pinned, too.

His eyes go wide, and I smile. "I'm not the shy kid that could be pushed around anymore. I defend what's mine, which includes friends and family." I tell him.

"Do you even know how much you cost me by blocking this

land developer? These guys are going to be pissed. You have no idea what you did!" He yells.

"Sadly, I don't care what they do to you." I hiss just as Nate and his partner, Dan, come running. I went to school with both of them and heard they joined the police department.

"Jasper, back up," Nate says, as he reaches my side.

My temper gets the best of me, and I slam his head against the wall hard, before letting go and taking a step back.

The next hour is spent explaining everything that happened, going over the video Brynn got, and talking about our meeting with the state.

According to Lin, she was at the front desk, helping the new girl learn the booking system. The same girl who called Kade and the cops. There was a couple upstairs yelling, and the sound of glass crashing, so Lin sent Dale up to deal with it, and Kade went with him.

Turns out, the husband was too handsy with a girl at the pool, and the wife threw the lamp at his head. There was lots of yelling and a few more items being thrown, before Kade and Dale got them separated enough to calm them down. Needless to say, they checked out early soon after.

During the time Dale and Kade were upstairs, is when the mayor came in. He was yelling all sorts of things about costing him money. Calling Lin a bitch and a whore, and then saying she and her friend were going to pay. Her friend being Brynn. I can tell by the rage in Kade's eyes he's just as pissed about hearing all this as I am.

Lin tried to back away to run upstairs, but the mayor stopped her, and that's when he slammed her against the wall, demanding to know who she fucked up at the capital to get the state to intervene.

Apparently, Brynn and I walked in right after that. The video was enough to get harassment and assault charges filed against the mayor. They'll also be looking into what the mayor was going on and on about with the land developers.

Once the cops leave, Kade takes Lin to their room, and I lead Brynn back to hers. Not a word is spoken on the walk there.

This is not how I thought our date would end.

* * *

Brynn

What the hell did the mayor mean about costing him money? He had to have meant the city money, right? Even then, I think the land developers would cost us more than they'd make us.

I push all that out of my head, as I let Jasper take me to my room. Instead, I focus on how he jumped right into action and defended Lin.

Once we're back in my room, I close the door and turn to look at him.

"Thank you," I tell him. Though, it feels so inadequate for how I'm feeling right now.

His face softens.

"You don't have to thank me, Firefly. Lin is a friend to both of us, and I know she's the closest thing to family you have, so that makes her important to me. There was no scenario where I didn't step in."

This man is the Jasper I fell in love with all those years ago, but so much better. He's aged perfectly, grown up, and only become greater. He's protective and sentimental. Sweet and caring, but he has a hard side for those that cross him. He still knows me, and I know, I know him, too.

He takes a step closer, and a million things are still running through my head.

"Don't you know I'd do anything for you?" He asks, before leaning down to kiss me. "Because I would, and because I still love you. I don't think I ever stopped." He kisses me again.

He loves me. I know he's shown it, but he just said it, and I don't know, if I can say it back. He leans in and kisses me again, and my brain short circuits. When it starts running again, I realize I'm ready. For him, and for us.

"I want you, Jasper, and I've never been surer of anything in my life. I want you and us. I want the dream we had back then, only I want to make it bigger and better." I tell him.

His eyes search mine, like he's waiting for me to say *'gotcha'* and tell him I'm just joking.

"I mean it," I whisper.

"Thank God." He says, before his mouth is back on mine. Only this kiss isn't soft and sweet, it's deep and frantic and filled with need. It's all the I love you's wrapped into a kiss. I kiss him back just as hard, because while I may not be able to say the words right now, I sure as hell can show him how I feel.

He walks me back towards my bed, all without taking his hands or his mouth off me. When the back of my knees hit the bed, I sit on the edge and look up at him.

He removes his shirt in that swift motion only guys can master, and his muscles bulge and twist, as he does, and my eyes are riveted on them. With his tan chest on full display, my eyes rake over him. He leans down and slowly starts lifting my top, giving me time to stop him, but I won't. I lift my arms, and he removes my top, and it joins his shirt on the floor.

While kissing me, he pushes me onto the bed and steps between my legs. He's careful to keep his weight off me, as he starts kissing my chest and along the cups of my bra, before reaching behind me to unhook it. He slowly pulls it away and tosses it to the floor.

"You are more beautiful than I remember. How is that possible?" He asks.

"Says the guy who grew muscles on top of his muscles." I smile and reach up to trail my hand down his chest. His skin and muscles flex under my touch.

He makes quick work of removing the rest of my clothes, and then stands back to look at every inch of me. If it was anyone else, I'd feel embarrassed, but the hunger in his eyes, tells me he likes what he sees.

"You have on too many clothes," I say with a smile.

He removes his clothes, before his knees hit the floor in front of me. His hands on the inside of my thighs push my legs wide, as he gets closer.

"I have been dreaming of this moment for so long, Firefly. I'm going to take my time." He says, as he runs his hands up my thighs to my hips and pulls my ass to the edge of the bed.

His hands rest on my lower belly, and his thumb starts to circle my clit. All I can do is close my eyes and let the sensation wash over me.

"Jasper." I can't seem to form the words I need to say, but he knows.

"Cum for me, Firefly." He says and starts fucking me with his tongue. There's no easing me into it. There's just him, taking what he wants, and it pulls my orgasm from me, faster than I thought possible. Before I know it, I'm cumming and screaming his name.

He kisses his way back up my stomach, between my breasts, and up my neck to my lips. I can still taste myself on him, and it's more erotic than I ever thought possible.

Jasper moves me up the bed, before standing and reaching into his pants for his wallet and pulling out a condom. He makes quick work of rolling it on, before he's back on the bed and climbing over me.

He kisses his way up my stomach again, but this time, nips at the underside of my breasts, before scraping his teeth on the sides of my rib cage, where he knows I'm ticklish. I start laughing and trying to pull away from him, as his kisses glide up my neck again.

"I love your laugh." He smiles, and it seems to have broken some of the tension.

"You sure about this, Firefly? We can wait as long as you want." He says.

"Never been surer of anything in my life," I say.

Bracing himself on his forearms, he leans down to kiss me, as he lines himself up. The head of his cock at my entrance makes me gasp. As he kisses me, he starts to slide into me, slowly thrusting, until his hips are flush against my thighs. Only then, does he break the kiss and pull back to look into my eyes for just a moment, before he squeezes his eyes shut and buries his head in my neck.

"You feel so fucking good." He groans and pulls back, thrusting in and out of me.

I can feel him drag along my walls, and the way he's angled hits my clit with each thrust. I wrap my legs around his waist

170

and pull him in even closer to me.

"I can feel you clenching me so tight. Firefly, you need to cum now." He grits out and moves a hand between us to put pressure on my clit.

A few hard strokes combined with his thrusting, and my orgasm overtakes me, and I'm screaming his name and holding on for dear life, like he's the only thing keeping me from falling off the edge of a cliff, because in that moment, he is.

Just as I come back to myself, I feel his whole body go stiff, and he groans my name. For a brief moment, I wish I could feel his release inside me. But the idea is out of my head, as soon as it entered.

He barely rolls to the side, before he collapses.

"Damn, I don't remember it being like that between us." He says.

"That makes two of us." I sigh.

He gets up and heads to the bathroom to clean up, before coming back to bed and pulling me to his side. I curl up with my head on his shoulder and my naked body pressed to his, and I can't imagine a more perfect moment. My world feels right again for the first time in a long time.

"You know, I read these books about couples who have sex on the beach, and all I can think about is how, when I walk the beach, I end up with sand everywhere. Can you imagine sex and getting sand *everywhere*? Then, what about sand crabs?" I say, and we both end up laughing.

He turns to his side and props himself on his elbow to look down at me. He just stares for a moment, before brushing some hair from my face. In bed with me relaxed, he's so beautiful.

"I love that we can laugh like this." He says.

I smile, "Me too."

Chapter 25

Jasper

Waking up with Brynn in my arms, is by far one of the best mornings of my life. Slipping from the bed, I stand and just watch her sleep for a while, before going to the kitchen to make her breakfast.

She has always loved my western omelets, so I make us both one, along with some breakfast potatoes, and of course, bacon and coffee.

When a flash of yesterday after our date comes to my head, and the fact that I didn't call my mom to tell her I wouldn't be home last night, I wince. Pulling out my phone that was on silent for our date, I groan.

Eight missed calls and over twenty-five text messages. Mostly, from my mom.

First, I shoot off a text to Kade, asking how Lin is. My guess is I won't hear back anytime soon, but whenever he sees the text, it's fine. Then, I read my mom's texts.

Mom: How's was your date with Brynn?

Mom: What happened with the mayor? Are you and Brynn

okay?

I cringe. I should have called my mom. Of course, she'd hear about it from someone else.

Mom: Boy, don't you dare go ignoring me now. You best call me soon as you get this.

Mom: Okay, if you aren't coming home at least call and let me know you aren't in jail.

Mom: Called the jail. Nate told me you were fine and not in jail.

This one makes me laugh, because I can see my mom calling and chewing out poor Nate about if I'm in jail or not. I know if I was there, my mom would have left my ass in there overnight, but she'd have been there with bail money in the morning.

A few more messages from my mom, including one of her trying to bribe me to call her, one telling me she called a poor, harassed Rich for details of where I was and upon finding out I was with Brynn, and then she sent me one reminding me she wanted a daughter-in-law *before* grandbabies.

The voice messages she left were pretty much along the same lines, just with some yelling mixed in.

I take a deep breath and ask one of the kitchen guys to finish up the breakfast potatoes for me, while I call her. I step into the kitchen office and call her back.

"Boy, you better be lying on your deathbed in some hospital room right now." Mom says, answering her phone.

"I'm sorry. I turned my phone on silent for my date, just like you taught me, too. When we got back to The Inn, we saw the mayor, and it all happened so fast. Then, we spent over an hour talking to the police, and Brynn was drained, so I took her to her room, and we fell asleep." I tell her.

"Tell me you at least used protection," Mom says, calling me out on the info I left out.

"Yes, Mom." I sigh.

"Good. Now, you okay?" She asks in a more calmly voice.

"Yeah, Lin was the one he put his hands on. I walked in and got to the mayor right before Kade did, so I'm the one who stopped him. Nate assures me there won't be a way for him to come after me, because I was protecting Lin. Either way, I'd do it again." I tell her.

"Damn right you would. You don't let any guy put his hands on a woman, especially those girls." She says in a stern voice.

"I know, Mom," I tell her.

"Well, you need to make it a point to call me, if you aren't going to be home. So, I at least know you're safe." She says.

I think of holding Brynn in my arms, like I did last night.

"Mom, I think it's safe to assume I won't be home at night and just be surprised, when I am, because I'm going to be attached to Brynn's hip for as long as she lets me," I tell her.

Mom grunts, but I know she's smiling. The guy in the kitchen gives me a sign the food is ready.

"I'm going to let you go, so I can go feed my girl. I love you Mom, and I'm sorry for worrying you." I tell her.

"Love you, too. I'm glad you're safe and happy."

We hang up, and I grab a tray to take the food to Brynn's room. The whole time I'm thinking of how great it is to have someone worry about me. I'm not thrilled to be living back home with my mom, but it's a nice change from the cold, lonely apartment I had in New York. I could go days without talking to someone on my days off, and here, I can barely go an hour.

It's a night and day difference, but I love life on The Island so much more now, cuddling my pillow. The thought makes me smile that even in her sleep she's reaching for me.

I set the tray down on the nightstand and sit on the edge of the bed. Pushing some hair from her face, I start trying to wake her up slowly.

"Time to get up, Firefly," I say in a soft voice.

My girl is not a morning person, so waking her, as gently as possible, is for the best.

When her eyes flutter open and land on me, my whole body warms. Just her look has me pinned in place, but when she smiles, my heart races.

She rolls over onto her back and stretches with her hands above her head. Her breasts are on full display, and I wonder if she's sore between her thighs.

My hand seems to have a mind of its own, as it reaches out and gives one of her firm globes a squeeze and rub my thumb across the stiff peak. She moans and arches her back, pushing her chest further into my hand.

My hand trails down her stomach and finds her core wet and her clit swollen.

"Were you dreaming of me?" I ask, as I play with her clit.

"Yes," she says a bit breathlessly.

"What was I doing in this dream?" I ask.

"The day I found you in the shower." She groans.

"Yeah?"

"I joined you." She says.

"Have this dream often?" I ask, slipping a finger into her.

"Every night."

"How about after we eat breakfast, we go make that dream come true?" I ask her.

"Yes," she groans.

I remove my fingers and bring them to my mouth, licking them clean.

"Jasper!" She whines.

"Eat, and then shower," I say, because I'm now hard as nails. "Sit up, Firefly. I made your favorite," her hazel eyes light up, as she sits up against the headboard.

"Is it a Western Omelet?" She asks.

"Yep, with breakfast potatoes and bacon," I say, handing her the cup of coffee.

"A girl can get used to this." She smirks, drinking her coffee.

"I want you to get used to it," I tell her, leveling her with my stare.

Every day for the rest of our lives I want to do this. Go to sleep with her in my arms, after we make love, and then wake up and make her breakfast, and then awaken her with an orgasm. Afterwards, we'll sit in bed and eat breakfast together, before we start our day. That's my dream.

I lean in to give her a chaste kiss, before handing her the plate of food. I take her fork and cut off the corner of the omelet and feed it to her.

"Mmm, I've missed your omelets. No one makes a western like you do." She moans.

Seeing her enjoying the food I made for her, has me turned on even more than I was last night.

She lets me feed her each bite, and it's an erotic dance, as her eyes stay on mine. The way her mouth wraps around her fork, and every now and then, her eyes roll back in her head, enjoying the food. When she's finished, I set the plate aside.

"My turn." She says and reaches for my plate.

She takes her time feeding me. By the time both plates are

clear, I'm hard as steel and have a wet spot on the front of my pants from the cum that has been leaking out.

"Shower with me, Firefly?" I ask, and she nods.

"Showering with you, is something I've always wanted to do, but we never got to it." She says.

"Me too," I say, and I follow her into the bathroom. My eyes glide to her heart-shaped ass, now completely naked.

This woman is going to be the death of me. A sweet, perfect death.

As she's turning on the shower, she looks over her shoulder at me and catches me staring at her and smirks. Then, she turns around and lets me get the full view, as she leans against the wall.

"Like what you see?" She asks, raising an eyebrow at me.

"I love what I see." I don't hide that I'm letting my eyes roam over her.

Wrapping my hands around her hips, I pull her close. Skin-to-skin was always my favorite thing with her, and now, I crave it more than I ever thought possible.

I look her in the eyes, and we both stand there entranced in each other.

"I love you, Firefly," I want to make sure she understands it.

In her eyes, I see the words she can't bring herself to say. She's still holding herself back, and that's fine, because I will prove myself.

"It's okay. You say it, when you're ready. I can love you enough for both of us. It doesn't mean I'm going to stop saying it, though."

"Good, I like hearing it." She says.

"Good, because I like saying it."

Just like that, playful Brynn is back, pulling me into the

shower with a smile on her face. And it's the best shower I have ever had.

Chapter 26

Brynn

It took two hours after that sexy as hell shower to get away from Jasper and make my way over to The Sunrise Inn to talk to Lin. I find them in her office. Kade is sitting in the office chair, and Lin is on his lap. They're so wrapped up in each other that they don't notice I'm standing right in the doorway.

I watch them for a minute, and Kade has Lin giggling. They're so happy, and I know without a shadow of a doubt I want that. I'm pretty sure Jasper is the guy who can give it to me. We just need to get there.

I knock on the door frame and smile.

"Brynn! Sorry." Lin tries to stand up, but Kade won't let her.

"It's fine," I wave a hand at them. "I was hoping to steal her away for lunch and some girl time. We need to catch up and talk about yesterday." I say.

Kade looks hesitant, like he doesn't want to let Lin out of his sight. After what happened, I can't blame him.

"We can camp out in your room and have Jasper bring us lunch there." I suggest.

Kade smiles, "I'd prefer that, if that's okay. I'm still on edge after yesterday." He admits.

"I figured. It took a miracle and a few promises to get Jasper to let me go and come here this morning." I smile.

Even though, Lin and Kade's room is right down the hall from the office, Kade still walks us to the door of their room and stands there to watch us make it safely inside.

"Have a good lunch, Goldie," Kade says and kisses her on her cheek.

Once the door is closed, I collapse on the couch.

"This is going to be so much harder to do, when you're living at your parents' house next season." I say.

"Well, we will just have to kick Kade out of the office, then," Lin says and plops down next to me.

"You guys make plans for the house, yet?" I ask, stalling a bit.

It's painful to think of doing more changes to those houses. We were almost unable to paint them and make them ready for vacation rentals. But now, they will get a full makeover. So many happy memories are in those houses.

Lin smiles and pulls her long, blonde hair up into a messy bun with the hair tie she has on her arm.

"There are two days at the end of July that no one booked. So, we blocked them out, and we're getting the contractor in and making all the plans. Kade is even hiring a designer to work with them. So, they can get in to see the space, and we can tell them what we want., After the season ends, and the weekend after Labor Day, they'll have it planned out and ready to go." She says.

When our parents died, we both kept our parents' houses, which are next door to each other. Renting them out, as vacation rentals pays for the mortgage on the houses and then some.

"Must be nice having a super-rich movie star husband." I joke.

"It is, but it's weird. I'm so used to watching every dime we spend, making sure every decision is profitable, and doing everything we can ourselves. It's different now. Kade is good with his money, and he doesn't spend it like crazy, but he does spoil me."

Lin is the one thing he doesn't care about spending money on. He's a bit tight with money for anything else, but when it comes to Lin, he doesn't think twice. Like making sure she had the perfect wedding dress.

"Good, I'd expect nothing else," I tell her.

"Okay, I know this isn't why you're here. Spill it." She says.

So, I do. I tell her about Jasper's surprise dinner on my porch; our talk on the beach. I tell her about our date yesterday; our trip down memory lane. The kiss. About finding her in the lobby, and Jasper taking me back to my room. I tell her about the sex, and Jasper's I love you. I tell her all of it, and her eye grows a little wider at each new thing I throw at her.

When I'm done, I take a big breath of air and blow it out.

"So, what do you think?" I ask her.

"I don't even know where to start. Do you love him?" She asks.

Leave it to Lin to go right to the jugular. I'm glad I thought about this, before I came over, because I know she won't let it go.

"Yeah, I never stopped," I whisper.

"But you're too scared to tell him." She says. Sometimes, it's kind of freaky how well your best friend knows you.

I just nod.

"It's okay. You'll tell him, when you're ready. I know Jasper, and he will wait. He's been waiting all this time for another chance, so he'll continue waiting." Lin says.

His face, when he says those three simple words, flashes through my mind. Though, he may be saying it with his mouth, it's his deep, brown eyes that show me he means it. Desire is written all over his face, as he stares at me unblinking, when he says it. It's so intense that I know he means it.

"Okay so, how are you?" I ask, needing to change the subject.

"Well loved." She says, and we both burst into giggles.

There's a knock on the door, before it opens, and Kade and Jasper peek their heads in.

"I love hearing that giggle, Goldie," Kade says to Lin.

"I second that, Firefly," Jasper says to me.

Both men have on matching crooked smiles that would melt the heart of every female across the county.

"We brought you lunch." Jasper says, as they pull in a cart of food. Enough food to feed all four of us, plus, a few more.

"All this is for us?" Lin says, reading my mind.

"Well, we wanted you to have choices. These two are for us, and we're going to eat in the office. There's dessert, too. Eat, and take your time. We have been keeping you away from each other, so we want you to catch up." Kade says.

"And get so fat that we can't get another guy ever again." I joke, which earns me glares from both guys. That only makes us both burst out laughing all over again.

The guys take their food and go back to the office. We dig into burgers, fries, loaded potato skins, and chocolate cake. There's also Jasper's sweet tea, so it's basically a perfect lunch.

"Okay, talk." I point my fork at her, and we start on the chocolate cake.

"Well, Kade wanted to make sure I was okay, so I had to strip, and of course, where I had the marks on my shoulders were red and a little sore. So, Kade took me to the bathroom, and we bathed together. He scrubbed every ounce of me clean three times." She says.

Flashes of the time Jasper washed me down in the tub in Raleigh flash through my mind, but I try to focus on Lin.

"So, then there was tub sex and talking and more sex and talking, and then shower sex and talking. I passed out at one point, and he woke me up twice, like he couldn't get enough of me, and he needed to know I was okay." Lin smiles.

"That's so sweet," I say.

"It is. He got up early to make sure the staff was doing their jobs, and everyone had breakfast and brought us breakfast in bed. Letting me sleep in, is one of my favorite things about him. He gets up early every day and tells me to go back to sleep. Most days, I get up with him, but some nights, he just tires me out too much." She giggles.

Watching Lin, I take in the huge smile on her glowing face. She looks more relaxed and so much happier with Kade around, and even more so now that they're married.

"So, how's married life?" I ask.

"I still don't think it's real. It feels like it did before, except now I have to remember to sign everything Linly Markson. Oh, and do you know how much of a pain in the ass it is to get your name changed on *everything*? My driver's licenses, my social security card, my bank account, the paperwork for The Inn, my car title, the house title, insurance, my phone bill, every fucking thing!" She shakes her head.

"Well, that's if I ever get married, then the man has to change his last name!" I joke.

"Seriously, I'd have kept my name if I knew!"

It's been a while, since we had a day like this, and by the time the guys join us for dinner, I'm feeling so much better. It's amazing what a good girl's night with your best friend can do. You can't buy therapy like that.

I leave that night with a promise to Lin to do this once a week.

Chapter 27

Jasper

Sitting in Lin's office, I look over at Kade, and I can tell he's as uneasy about this meeting as I am.

Nate called this morning and said he needed to talk to us about the mayor's case, and Kade was able to get him to agree to meet us here, instead of the station.

Kade is sitting in the leather chair behind the desk, and Lin is on his lap. He's holding her to him a little tighter than normal.

I'm sitting on the couch with Brynn pulled to my side, as close as she can possibly get. I'm beginning to understand why Kade has Lin on his lap, when Nate walks in wearing his police uniform. It's a sign this is a work call, and not a friendly one.

He greets us, and then closes the door and sits down in one of the empty chairs.

"So, we did some digging. There was no reason for the mayor to go off the way he did. It didn't make sense, when what you did about Main Street is good for the town. Something didn't sit well with me about him ignoring what the town wanted and pushing this development."

Nate shifts in his seat. "Looks like the mayor was going to get a big payday for himself for putting the land contract through. Upwards of the high six figures." Nate says.

Kade curses under his breath. "That's why he put a stop on the villa's permits, trying to get us to back down." He says.

"Yep. The paperwork is in process, and he's being removed from office. He was taking all sorts of bribes from people out of town, and he wasn't even hiding them. As soon as the paperwork is complete, the interim mayor will be put into place." Nate says.

"Who is that?" I ask.

"Josh." Nate smiles.

"The metal detector guy?" Kade asks.

"That's him," Nate confirms.

Josh is known for working at the bank his whole life. He's now semi-retired and working there just two days a week. The rest of his time is spent metal detecting on the beaches on the island, especially after storms.

"Well, then there shouldn't be any issues getting the villa's moving," Brynn says.

"Agreed," Lin says.

"The mayor, well he isn't the mayor anymore, so we'll have to go back to calling him, Bert." Nate shakes his head. "Anyway, Bert was given bail, but he hasn't posted it. There is a good chance he won't, but just in case, I wanted to let you know. If he posts bail, everyone knows to inform you. He isn't allowed to leave The Island, until the trial."

"Oh, fun," Kade says dryly.

I know what he's thinking. He will probably be right back here if he posts bail. We both need to take precautions if that happens. He's not normally a bad guy, but when people get backed in a corner, you just never know.

Nate says his goodbyes and leaves, but the four of us don't move.

"I don't want you sleeping alone," I tell Brynn without thinking.

"I haven't been." She chuckles.

"I'm also not sure I want to leave my mom alone, if Bert gets out." I think out loud.

"I'll get some extra security here and station someone outside her house. You don't have to tell her, if you don't want, too." Kade says.

I shake my head. "I have too, she'd notice."

"Yeah, she would," Brynn laughs.

Brynn's laugh is what I needed to pull me out of this funk that Nate's news left me in.

"Go for a walk with me, Firefly?" I ask her.

She nods and stands up. After saying goodbye to Lin and Kade, we head out to the beach hand-in-hand. She's quiet for a few minutes, before she starts talking.

"I think Josh will better for the town. But it's only six months, before we will be electing a new mayor." She says.

"I wonder if Kade is still interested in running. Though, I think he'd have a hard time going up against Josh." I say.

Kade is liked, but Josh is a local and liked just as much. So, if it came to it, I think the town would vote for a local, before they'd vote for someone so new to the area.

"I think the only reason Kade was talking about running was to get Bert out of office. If Josh does a good job, I don't think Kade has any interest in it." She says.

I nod my head in agreement.

"Here's to hoping we can finally move on with the villas,

though. I'd like to have them up, before next season, and be able to work out the kinks in the off season." She says.

"Knowing Kade, he'll make it happen the second he has the green light to do it. He would move mountains to make Lin happy, and Lin will agree with you on having any problems worked out, before the season." I tell her, giving her hand a squeeze.

When she looks up at me and smiles, I couldn't stop myself from leaning in and kissing her, if my life depended on it. She kisses me back with a smile on her face.

That smile is still there, when she pulls back. I know that look, playful Brynn is about to come out. It's also a smile that warns me to be on guard.

She wastes no time in proving me right, when she runs ahead of me a few feet, and then turns back and kicks her foot through the water, sending a spray of water at me, soaking my shirt.

I rush forward and grab her around the waist and lift her over my shoulder.

"You're going to pay for that!" I say, as I spin her around with her ass in the air.

When I set her down, the guy she had a date with, Daniel, is standing on the back steps of The Sunset Inn, watching us with a look I don't like on his face.

Brynn must follow my line of sight, because she sighs.

"What's he doing here?" She mumbles more to herself, but I still feel the need to remind her she's mine.

"Probably wants another date," I say, as she looks at me. "What are you going to tell him, Firefly?"

She gets an evil look on her face. "Well, not what I want, too. My mom would come back from the dead just to whoop my ass." She smirks.

"You are mine," I growl.

She pats my arm and turns to head over to see what he wants, but I grab her arm and pull her back to me.

Then, I stake my claim. I kiss her, and my body only relaxes, once she melts into me and kisses me back. She knows what I'm doing, and she's letting me be a caveman.

"I've been yours from day one." She says, pulling back with a smile and winking, before turning to go see what Daniel wants.

I follow not too far behind her. After the events from the other day with the mayor, Bert, I'm not ready to let her out of my sight just yet.

"Hey, Daniel. Anything I can help you with?" She says in her formal work voice.

I walk past them and sit on the wicker couch and pull out my phone, pretending to be doing something else. I have no idea what is even on my screen, because all I focus on is them.

"Oh well, I was out-of-town, getting the rest of my stuff from school, when I had heard about what happened with Bert and all, so I wanted to come and check on you," Daniel says, as his eyes keep darting over to me.

"I'm fine. Thank you, Daniel." Brynn says.

"I was also hoping for another date, but…" Daniel says.

"Sorry, but Jasper and I are back together." She says, and I don't even hide the smirk on my face.

Daniel nods. "Guess it's easier to date, when he's right here all the time."

I narrow my eyes at him. I didn't like his tone with that one. So, I stand up and move to Brynn's side, wrapping my arm around her waist.

"Also helps we have a history," I tell him, smiling.

He gives us a strained smile, before nodding.

"Well, I wish you two the best. See you around." He says and heads back inside towards the lobby.

When the door closes, Brynn turns in my arms to look at me.

"You didn't have to do that." She says, fighting a smile.

"I didn't like his tone." He says.

"Jasper, even if there was no you, I wouldn't have accepted a second date. I was so freaking bored." She groans and buries her head in my chest.

I pull her close and kiss the top of her head.

"Well, there is me, and I'm not going anywhere. You are kind of stuck with me. But Lin will pay for setting you up on that date." I tell her.

She giggles, but I feel it against my chest more than I hear it.

"Let's go in and get ready for The Sunset event," I say.

It's gotten even bigger, since we can now use the beach for it. Each one is different, so we have to adjust to make sure everything is set up.

But it's all worth it, because during every event, I get to hold Brynn, as we watch the sun go down. It's my favorite way to end each day.

Chapter 28

Brynn

The season is in full swing, and it seems each day blends into the next. Jasper always finds ways to spend time with me, no matter how busy we are. Then, every night, he's in my bed. He's even taken over part of my closet.

It's been over a week, since Nate came to tell us about Bert, the former mayor. Josh has now taken over as interim mayor and has approved our permit for the villas. We will break ground at the end of July, which is the middle of the season.

Kade made the contractor promise not to mess with the beach, so we can continue doing The Sunset events. We just have to go around the long way via the beach. I don't think guests will complain about a walk alongside the ocean.

I just finished a meeting with the contractor, Kade, and Lin, when I walk back into the lobby, and I'm not prepared to have the breath knocked out of me.

I find Jasper, sitting on one of the couches next to a boy, who can't be more than thirteen. Their backs are to me, allowing me to lean on the registration desk and listen to them.

"I'm here with my dad and his new girlfriend." The boy says.

"They forgot about me and went on some all-day boat trip."

My heart breaks for this boy. The father should be soaking up all the time he can get with his son.

"Well, I'm the chef here, and we're about to get ready to serve lunch. Would you like to come with me and see how a real kitchen works?" He asks.

The kid turns to look at Jasper, and even from here, I can see his whole face light up.

Jasper is so good with kids. How did I forget this? Though, he may be an only child, he was always around kids. He helped his mom with the daycare in church many times, and even babysat the twin boys down the street, when he was in high school. He would tutor kids in school, and while he wasn't ever on the football team, he liked to help the football players train.

When Jasper and the boy stand up, he spots me and smiles. I smile back and just shake my head and make my way to my office to get some work done.

An hour later, I can't stop thinking about that kid and Jasper's offer to help in the kitchen. I give up the pretense of working and head into the kitchen.

"Hey, how's it going?" I ask.

"Julian here is a natural in the kitchen." Jasper nods his head to the boy, who is stirring something in a large bowl. "Julian, this is Miss Brynn, she owns The Inn."

"Wow, you own this place?" Julian's eyes light up.

"Yep. My parents started it, before I was born, and I took over about five years ago." I tell him.

No point in getting into the heavy of why I took over. That's not what this kid needs today.

"My dad's job is boring. He does something with stocks in

the city. I never get to see him." Julian's eyes drop.

"But you're having fun in the kitchen?" I try to lighten the mood.

"Yeah! I got to learn how to prep for lunch. I've been able to make some sandwiches, and Mr. Jasper even let me create my own sandwich and put it out for today's special." He says.

"Yeah, what is it?" I ask.

"I call it the Sand Dollar Club. It's got turkey, bacon, Swiss cheese, herbed mayo, lettuce, tomato, and black olives on a toasted..." He trails off.

"Brioche bun." Jasper finishes for him.

"Yeah, he let me try the different buns to see which I liked best. We even put a little garlic butter on top, before toasting it." He says.

"It's been selling well, too." Jasper adds.

"Well, you've sold me. I'm staying, so I'll have a Sand Dollar Club." I tell him and take my seat on the stool to the side of the kitchen.

Julian's entire face lights up. He starts pulling out what he needs. Jasper toasts the bun, and Julian compiles the sandwich. Then, Jasper adds fries and his homemade pickles I love, and Julian brings it over to me. A moment later Ken drops a sweet tea in front of me with a wink and is back out in the dining room, before I can speak.

Both Jasper and Julian stare at me, waiting to hear what I think, and I feel like I'm on one of those reality TV shows that my last chef left me for. I take my time studying it.

"Presentation is excellent. It makes me hungrier just looking at it. I think it would make a great social media photo." I wink, pulling out my camera and taking a few photos to post later.

Then, I take a bite. I will say I've never had people watch me so intently before.

As I start to chew, I realize this kid has some amazing talents. It's honestly one of the best sandwiches I've ever had. That includes the one's Jasper and his dad have made me.

"This is really good, and even better than the stuff Jasper has made me before. Maybe, you need to give him sandwich making lessons." I say, taking another bite.

Julian stands a bit taller and smiles. His sun kissed tan skin glows, and his blue eyes sparkle.

"You have a lot of talent. Keep learning, go to school, and when you graduate, look me up. I'd gladly give you a job." Jasper says.

He then gives him a card that has both his restaurants on it, and they talk about what it's like running two restaurants, and why he's working at The Sunrise, as they finish up the lunch rush, and I eat my lunch.

Jasper looks up over at me from time-to-time, like he's checking to make sure I'm still here and doing okay. I like being in his space and being close to him. When I look at the counter I'm sitting next to, I notice no one uses it. I could set up my laptop here and work from here now and then. Especially, on days like today, where I can't seem to concentrate in my office.

Julian is so excited to be in the kitchen he even stays to help clean up after lunch, before going in search of his dad.

I try to work in my office again, but it just isn't happening, so I grab my laptop and head to the kitchen and set up on the counter, where I was at lunch. I start working and answering emails. I'm so engrossed in my work that I don't notice Jasper, walking up behind me.

"I like you working here in my kitchen." He says next to my

ear, wrapping his arms around my waist.

My whole body warms at that comment, though I'm not sure what to say. I decide to tease him a bit.

"Oh, your kitchen, huh? Last I checked, it was my kitchen." I smile up at him.

He leans down and kisses me, before smiling at me.

"But I am the chef here, which makes everything in it my responsibility, so that makes it my kitchen." He says.

"Oh, really?" I ask.

"Yes, really. That's kitchen basics 101, ask anyone." He says.

I just shake my head. "You sure I'm okay here? I couldn't seem to concentrate in my office today, but here, I'm getting a lot of work done."

"I love having you here. Something about having you close calms me." He says.

"That's how I feel, too," I tell him, and his eyes lock with mine. This is the closest I've come to telling him how I feel, and we both know it.

The dinner service flies by, and before I know it, they are finishing up cleaning the kitchen, and I can't remember the last time I got so much work done.

"Good workday?" Jasper asks, coming to my side.

"Yes, I caught up on emails, and not only posted to social media for both Inns, but got posts scheduled for the next two weeks. I updated the website, caught up on the books, approved all the inventory reports, and pulled some design ideas for the villas." I tell him, closing my laptop.

"Ready to get out of here?"

"Yes, but I'm thinking more of snuggling in bed than going out on the town," I tell him.

"Perfect, because that's just what I had in mind, too." He

196

says.

"Great minds think alike and all that," I say.

Once in my room, I collapse on my bed.

"You sure I wasn't in your way in the kitchen?" I ask again.

He doesn't answer me, as he lies down beside me and rolls over on top of me, pinning me to the bed.

"I loved having you there, Firefly, and in fact, I'm going to insist you be there more often. If you were in the way, I would tell you, because I don't want you to get hurt. I promise, you were in the perfect spot." He says, nipping at my neck.

"Okay." I gasp, as we start playing around.

He always knows how to take my mind off things and refocusing them. Orgasms do that.

Chapter 29

Jasper

I'm finishing up my weekly food order, when my mom calls. It's been a few days, since I have been home to see her, and I instantly feel guilty.

"Hey, Mom," I answer.

"I'm making dinner tonight." She says.

In Mom's language, that means I better be there, because she has something to talk to me about.

"I'll be there Mom and will even bring dessert," I tell her, trying to bribe her a bit.

"Sounds good. See you at six." She says.

That gives me two hours. Nothing like short notice, but my mom knows I'd drop anything for her, if she needs me, no notice needed.

I head out to find Brynn in her office. I tap lightly on the door frame to get her attention.

She looks up and smiles.

"Hey, how's your day going?" She asks.

"Good, so far. Mom called and wants me home for dinner. I guess, she needs to talk. Why don't you see if you can do dinner with Kade and Lin and catch up with them? I'll be back tonight."

"You know you can stay with your mom tonight. She probably misses you."

"I'm not sleeping without you in my arms. If you want me to stay at my mom's house, you better be coming with me." I tell her.

"You know she won't allow that." Brynn shakes her head.

"Then, I'll be back after dinner. Don't fight me on this."

"I'll be waiting." She takes a deep breath and reaches for something in her desk drawer, before standing up and walking over to me.

She holds her hand out to me, and in it, is a key.

"What's this?" I ask her.

"It's a key to my room. You've been staying here every night, and you work your butt off. I thought it might be a good idea." She shrugs her shoulders, but she won't look me in the eyes.

This small gesture means the world to me. It's a big step for her. I know this, and I'm not going to waste it.

I take the key with one hand and hook my other hand around her waist, pulling her into me.

"Thank you, Firefly. I'll use it tonight." I whisper against her lips right before I kiss her.

She wraps her arms around my neck and sinks into me. It's the best feeling in the world, and one I don't know how I went so long without.

She pulls back and runs her hands down my chest.

"Now, go have dinner with your mom. I'll see you tonight." She says.

I kiss her cheek, and then head out. I stop at the kitchen and grab one of the pies we made yesterday. Even though, all

I want to do is walk, I take my car. All the good walking paths are packed with tourists this time of year, and I don't want to deal with them.

I pull into my mom's drive away, and before I even get to the front porch, the smell of her cooking fills the air. It feels like home. Smiling, I jog up the front porch steps and go inside.

"Mom?" I call.

"Kitchen!" She yells back.

I slip off my shoes and head her way, setting the pie down on the counter.

"What are you making?" I ask.

"Meatloaf with a sage gravy, mashed potatoes, bacon, green beans, and rolls." She says, as she stirs the pot on the stove.

"All of Dad's favorites," I say more to myself than anything. Then, it hits me. Sometimes, my mom says the exact same thing.

"I figured it was only right with the one year anniversary of his passing coming up. Plus, I had a craving for this gravy something fierce." She says.

I barely make it to one of the bar stools, before my legs collapse. How did I forget it's next week? I didn't forget. I just wasn't thinking of it, because I've been so wrapped up in Brynn.

"Oh, Jasper, this wasn't to make you sad. You have been so happy, and that's all I want for you. But I figured we'd do something to celebrate your dad together, and also, I wanted to chat. Plus, I hadn't seen you for a bit."

She hasn't seen me, because I've been spending so much time with Brynn. Because I've been spending time with Brynn, there were no more nightly talks, when I get home, no more dinners, or breakfasts.

"I'm sorry, Mom. I will come home more, I promise." I tell her.

"Oh posh, I'm so happy you and Brynn are together. Just bring her over to dinner more. Gives me another reason to cook!"

I nod, but don't say anything. I can't talk, because of the lump in my throat. My mind works on autopilot, as I help Mom set the table and bring the food over. She talks about the girls at church, but I don't hear any of it.

It feels like my heart is being ripped out. I'm missing my dad so much right now, and knowing Brynn went through this, and I wasn't here for her, is killing me. How the hell was she ever able to forgive me? I can't forgive myself.

"So, I was thinking, why don't we take a picnic to the arch rock. It was your dad and my favorite date spot. We can have lunch there, and then visit him, and you can still get back to The Inn for the dinner rush. Will that work?" Mom asks.

"Yeah." I croak out.

Mom looks at me and purses her lips, before she starts talking about town gossip again.

"Hey, Mom. I'm going to go for a walk," I tell her, after dinner.

"Thank you for coming over for dinner." She hugs me.

"I'll be back." I try to smile.

I make my way to the graveyard, wanting to be close to my dad. I can't believe it's been almost a year. In a way, it doesn't feel like it's been that long. So much has happened, that in other ways, it's hard to believe it's only been a year.

He'd be so happy Brynn and I are working things out. He always thought of her as a daughter. I know he looked after her once I left. Thinking back to that time and knowing a fraction of what she went through, I can't imagine having lost both parents at the same time.

Damnit, I should have been there for her. I have thought about it before, and even said the words, but the emotion behind them has never been this strong. My eyes mist over, as I walk through the graveyard gates.

I make my way over to the side, and at the last minute, change direction and head to Brynn's parents' graves.

This is the first time I've visited, since the funeral. I kneel down and place a hand on the shared tombstone.

"I'm so sorry I wasn't there for her, like I should have been. She needed me, and I failed her. I failed you. After everything you guys did for me, I failed you. I hope you can forgive me. She seems to have forgiven me, but I have no idea how." I say, as my tears fall.

I bend my head towards the ground and take a few deep breaths, hoping they understand everything I can't seem to say.

"Jasper." I hear what I swear sounds like my dad's voice.

I look up and see no one around me. The sun is starting to set, but even in the shadows, I don't see anyone. When I look back down at the ground, I hear it again.

"Jasper." It's almost like a whisper.

Jerking my head up, I look around, but still see no one. I lean in and kiss Brynn's parents' tombstone, and then head over to my dad's grave.

The air feels colder here, but as odd as it is, I swear it feels like he's standing there with me.

"We miss you every damn day, Dad. I can't believe it's been a year. I moved home, and then made things right with Brynn. By the grace of God, she's forgiven me and given me a second chance. One I don't deserve, and I realize that now more than ever. Mom is doing a lot better than I expected and seems to be enjoying her time at church and fueling the town gossip, as much as possible. I think she's happy to have me home."

I pause, trying to think of what to say, and of how to voice my emotions. "I will make you proud. That's a promise I can make. I will take care of Mom, just like you would have. I'm sorry I wasn't here to give you one last hug and tell you how much I loved you."

Then, I break down and cry. I didn't realize how much I hated that I wasn't here to say goodbye and see him one last time, before he passed. I should have been. There was no reason for me to be in New York anymore. We both knew it, but he never pushed. He hinted, but never pushed.

When I finally get my emotions under control, I make my way back to my mom's house, and on the way, I text Brynn.

Me: I'm going to stay at my mom's tonight. Good night, Brynn.
Brynn: Everything okay?
Me: Yes. Just a long night. See you tomorrow.
Brynn: Good night, Jasper.

When I get home, Mom is sitting in the living room reading. Her nightly routine for as long as I can remember.

"What's wrong?" She looks up at me.

"Just went and talked to Dad. I'm going to crash here tonight." I tell her.

Her face softens. "You let Brynn know?" She asks.

"Yeah, she knows."

"Okay. I'll make breakfast in the morning. Any special

203

requests?" She asks.

"Dad's Caribbean tropical pancakes?"

Mom knows how to make almost all of Dad's recipes. She may not be a chef, but she can read a recipe card better than anyone I know. He made sure to write every recipe down for her.

"I haven't had that in years. It's perfect. See you in the morning."

I give her a kiss and go to bed. Dad was always trying new recipes, and my mom was his taste tester. The pancakes have tropical fruit with a fruit syrup, some spices, and honey butter. It was his way of pulling tourists into the beach vacation experience, as he called it.

As I'm getting ready for bed, I realize I haven't created any new recipes for the restaurants, since I've been home. The menu has been pretty much the same, other than the specials, for over a year now. I've been so wrapped up in working at The Sunset.

When was the last time I even checked into the restaurants? Two or three weeks? Maybe more? But the thought of working in any other kitchen other than The Sunset doesn't sit well with me either.

I need to get things in order and better manage this legacy my dad left me. No matter what it takes, I will make him proud. I won't let him down again.

Chapter 30

Brynn

I can feel Jasper pulling away a little more each day, and I'm not sure why. It started the night after he had dinner with his mom. His texts were short, but the next day, he was just cold. It was like he was going through the motions of what he had to do.

He smiled, when he should. Hugged me, kissed me, but the spark wasn't there. When I'd ask him about it, he'd shake his head and say he was fine.

He stopped staying in my room. He's been staying with his mom every night, since that dinner. I want to know what happened, but I want him to know I trust him, too.

I'm sitting at my desk and thinking of Jasper and trying to figure out what caused this. I'm tapping a pencil on my desk, lost in thought. Was it giving him the key? Was it too much? I didn't think it would be. He was saying *'I love you,'* while I couldn't say it, but I was showing him. This is the guy who says how much he loves me and is okay with me not saying it back. I thought a key would show him what he means to me. He hasn't used it once.

The pencil flips out of my hand and lands by my calendar at the corner of the desk. That's when I notice the day. His dad's one year anniversary of the day he died is coming up. I bet his mom brought it up, because she wanted to do something. Lin and I still do something each year, and this year will make six years.

I make my way into the kitchen and watch him work. He looks at me, and while his eyes meet mine, they are emotionless. A week ago, his whole face would light up, when he saw me, and he'd come over and hug me. He'd ask if I ate, and then try to feed me, even if I had. Today? Nothing. He just goes right back to work.

So, I call over to him. "Can we go for a walk?" I ask him.

"Not now, Brynn, I'm getting ready for the dinner service." He says, his voice flat.

That's another thing. He's stopped using my nickname and calls me Brynn all the time. I kind of hate it more and more each day.

"That wasn't a request. It was more of an employer to employee demand," I say.

I will play dirty to get him alone for just a few minutes to talk. Thankfully, it works. He stops what he's doing, washes his hands, and takes off his apron.

"You have a choice. We can walk on the beach, or we can talk in my office." I offer him.

"Your office." He says, almost sounding annoyed.

Once in my office, I close the door and sit next to him on the couch, but I don't touch him.

"What's going on with you?" I ask.

"Nothing." He says.

"Well, your mood sucks. You're draining the kitchen staff.

My staff who was all smiles and laughter a week ago is afraid to even talk in the kitchen. The dining room staff is picking up on, and it has to stop. So, I'm going to ask you again, what's wrong?"

He sighs but looks out of the window, instead of at me and says nothing. Okay, time to rip the Band-Aid off.

"Is all this because your dad's anniversary is coming up?" I ask.

The tick in his jaw tells me I'm right.

"Okay, well, you have trained the kitchen staff well. We can do without you for a bit. Heck, I have a stack of applications I can still go through. You don't need to be here, Jasper. Go where you are needed. Where you want to be, because you sure don't want to be here." I tell him, even though, I hate the idea of not seeing him every day.

"I want to be here." He says still looking out of the window.

"No, you don't. I don't know what is going on. I have an idea, but you can't keep draining the mood from my kitchen. You keep pushing me away; putting up more walls than I had. Fine, take your time, and we'll deal with this in a few weeks. But I can't wait a few weeks to get my kitchen back in order. If you want to be here, then *be* here. Or tell me to go through the applications and find someone. Why don't you go home and spend some time with your mom?" I say.

His jaw ticks again, before he stands.

"Fine." He grits out and walks out of the door without looking back.

I collapse against the back of the couch and fight the tears that flood my eyes.

I shoot off a quick text to his mom, saying Jasper is in a bad mood, and I sent him home. I figure I owe her a heads-up at least. I toss my phone on my desk, before going into the kitchen.

"Hey, guys. I told Jasper to head home. He has some personal stuff going on. So, we need to pull together without him. Can we do that?" I ask.

"Don't worry, Miss Brynn, we got this," Tony says. He's the sous chef and has been Jasper's right-hand guy, since he's been here.

"Okay, any problems call me," I say, before walking out.

I go to find Lin and Kade. Lin is talking to someone at the front desk. I make eye contact with her and tilt my head towards her room, and she nods. So, I head over there. Before she was married, I'd have used my key and just wait on her, but now, I knock.

Kade opens the door, takes one look at me, and steps back to let me in.

"Lin will be here in a few minutes. She's talking to someone in the lobby," I tell him, while taking a seat on the couch and throwing my head back to look at the ceiling.

"Jasper?" He says.

"Yep," I say, popping the p.

"Okay, I'm here," Lin says, a bit breathless.

"Boy issues. I think I'll head out." Kade says.

"No, stay you need to hear this. Maybe, you can help him." I say.

Lin and Kade sit down on the love seat and turn to face me.

"The anniversary of his dad's death is coming up next week, and he's in a bad place. He's pushing me away, he's shut down, and he's emotionless. I sent him home, because he was scaring the kitchen staff. He has been ignoring me ever since that dinner with his mom. I'm losing him, and I feel it. I just don't know why. If it's the stuff with his dad, I can wait it out, but I think it's more than that." I say.

"He needs time. You remember that first year it was really hard. Hell, last year, was hard, and it's been five years. I don't think he completely dealt with it, before coming home. I think he got involved with you and forgot, and now, he's mad he forgot to be upset." Lin says.

"I know it was hard for us, but I guess, I don't remember shutting down like he is," I say.

"We weren't able, too. We were trying to learn a business and get on track. When we got too low, we had each other pointing it out. Nor did we have another parent to take care of. We didn't have anyone but each other, and we knew exactly what the other was going through. Give him time and be there for him, even when he pushes you away." Lin says.

"From a guy's point of view, we don't want our girl to see us weak. We are supposed to be the protector, and the strong one, when things go bad. So, it's probably just as hard on him. He doesn't want to need you, but he does. He won't admit it, because he wants to look strong to you." Kade says.

"Then what do I do?" I ask.

"Wait it out. More than likely, after the anniversary passes, things will get easier." Kade says.

"If it doesn't?" I ask.

"Then, the three of us get with his mom and push him," Lin says.

"I've never been good at waiting," I say.

"Oh, I know." Lin laughs.

"Great, so let's wait." I sigh.

My gut is screaming at me that there's more and waiting is a bad idea. I should have listened.

Chapter 31

Brynn

I'm trying to keep busy, because this whole waiting things out plan isn't working for me. I figure if I can keep busy, I won't have the need to corner Jasper and go off on him and try to shake him out of this funk he's in.

When my phone rings, I lunge for it, welcoming the distraction.

"Hello?" I ask, kicking myself for not checking the caller ID first.

"Brynn, dear, I was wondering if you have time to meet me for lunch?" Jasper's mom asks.

"Sure, Mrs. Adams. Where were you thinking?" I ask, as I pull up my calendar.

"Well, today if possible. Jasper went into work at Samuel's, and I'd rather talk, when he isn't here." She says.

Samuel's is his restaurant. It the fancier one known for its southern twist on seafood.

"Of course, I can be there in half an hour."

"Perfect, see you then, dear." She says.

As soon as we hang up, I call Lin.

"Hey, keeping busy?" Lin answers.

"I was trying, and then Jasper's mom called and invited me over for lunch today," I tell her.

"I wonder what she wants," Lin says.

"I have no idea, but I plan to find out. You watch The Inn for me, while I'm gone?" I ask.

"Of course! But I expect all the details, when you get back." She says.

"Of course!" I try to mimic her enthusiasm, and judging by the look on Lin's face, I failed.

Once off the phone with her, I send a text to Rich, letting him know I will be stepping out for a bit and to call Lin, if he needs anything. Then, I go to my room to get ready. I know she won't care what I wear, but I feel like this is important, so I want to dress up a bit. A sundress and some strappy sandals will do the trick. I touch up my hair and makeup, before I head out.

As I pull down the familiar street, I worry what she has to say might not be good news. Parking in the driveway, I start to miss Jasper something fierce.

The front door is open, so I tap on the screen door.

"Mrs. Adams?" I call out.

"Come on in, dear. I'm just finishing up the sandwiches!" She calls from the kitchen at the back of the house.

I head in, making sure to take my sandals off.

"Oh, look how beautiful you are in that dress. Please, tell me you're going to walk down Main Street and be seen after this!" She says.

"Of course!" I laugh. Though, I hadn't planned on it, but why not. I can get some donuts for Lin and me, while I tell her about this lunch.

Once we're seated, she wastes no time with what she wants to talk about. Of course, it's about Jasper.

"So, the other night he came over for dinner, and we talked about the one year anniversary of his dad's passing coming up. I thought we'd plan something and spend the day together. What I hadn't planned on was throwing him into this funk."

"That was the first night he stayed back here, huh?" I ask more to myself.

"Yep." She looks at me, waiting for me to add in my two cents.

"Well, since that day, he's kept me at arm's length. I sent him home the other day, because he was scaring my kitchen staff. My staff who like to talk and joke and always have smiles on their faces were scared to make a sound. He's going through the motions, when he's with me. Hug, kiss, but he isn't seeing me. He isn't there." I sigh.

"I've noticed it, too. It's the same, when he's here at home. Then, last night, he comes home from working dinner shift at the bar and pours himself a drink. Well, a few drinks. Then, he starts rambling about how he doesn't know how you forgave him, because he can't forgive himself. Then, he said it was no wonder you haven't said I love you yet, when he tells you." She says, giving me a soft look.

I know my cheeks are red, as I can feel the heat.

"I've been hesitant, yeah. He walked away last time, and now, I feel like he's walking away again. Did he tell you the day of that lunch I gave him a key to my place? I've never done that, and Lin is the only other person who has a key. I was trying to show him little by little."

"No, he didn't tell me." She shakes her head.

"He promised to come over that night after dinner with you,

but texted and said he was staying here. The next day, it was like he had checked out." I say.

"Tomorrow, is the anniversary, and he's decided to go out fishing, like he and his dad used to do." She says and eyes me.

My blood runs cold. He's going out on the water in a fishing boat.

Just like my parents.

I clamp my eyes closed and turn my head down, as my heart races. Panic fills me at the thought of him out on the water. The same water that took my parents the same way, after a day of fishing.

"Oh, Brynn. Does he know how you feel about all this?" She asks.

"He knows I haven't been back in the water and won't go in the ocean. Anyway, I doubt he'd care how I felt about him going on the water. I'm sorry I need to go." I say, standing.

I know I'm being rude, we aren't done with lunch, and we are in the middle of a conversation, but I can't stay here. I don't remember leaving her house or the drive back to The Inn. But the next thing I know, I'm in my room and lying on my bed crying, and I can't stop.

I don't know how long I cry, but when I open my eyes, my head hurts, my eyes hurt, my heart hurts, and the sun is setting. I must have drifted off.

So, I text Lin.

Me: SOS! My room.

I know that's all I have to say. We don't send SOS messages often, but when we do, it's bad. My guess is she will probably bring Kade with her.

A few minutes later, I'm proven right, as she uses her key and lets herself in with Kade right behind her.

"Oh, Brynn." Lin sighs and climbs into bed with me. I scoot back just enough, so she can lay down facing me. Kade sits on the other side of me with his back to the headboard.

"Jasper's…" I start crying again. "Going…fishing…tomorrow." I choke out. "On a… boat." I sob. Thankfully, Lin is the one person in the whole world who understands why I'm so upset. On the anniversary of his dad's death, he's going to go fishing on a boat in the same water that has claimed our parents' lives.

I'm terrified, and I'm pissed he's shutting me out. I'm hurt more than anything, and I don't know how to deal with any of it.

"It's going to be okay," Lin says, wrapping me in her arms.

"It's not. I've had this gut feeling for weeks and now this. Lin something bad is coming. I feel it."

They don't say a word. Not that they would know what to say. Thankfully, they don't leave me alone either. Lin stays in bed with me just like in old times, and Kade takes the couch.

It's great to have a family, even when your world is crashing down around you.

Chapter 32

Jasper

The sun is barely up, and I'm already out at the docks. Pretty much everyone on The Island has learned how to drive a boat at an early age and got their boating license, as soon as they could.

My dad and I always loved to go out fishing on a quiet morning with a thermos full of coffee, some donuts, and enjoy the peace and quiet. My favorite days were, when the water was calm and smooth as glass, like it is today. There's a little fog in the air that gives a slightly creepy atmosphere.

I park the boat at the place my dad swears he always caught the most fish. I don't even cast my line, as I just sit here and remember mornings much like these with my dad. He loved catching fresh fish, and then bringing them home to try a new recipe. He went shrimping once and caught so much he invited the whole block over for a shrimp fry. It was a fish fry, but with shrimp.

He loved to feed people, especially those he loved. My mom and I were at the top of that list and later Brynn.

Brynn.

My heart aches just thinking of her name. The perfect girl who is way too good for me. She has to know it too, but yet, she still let me in her life and in her bed. I've loathed going to bed alone these last few nights, but I hate the way I feel around her now.

Damn, she sent me home from my own kitchen. Was I really that bad? Lord, help me, I was, wasn't I?

I cast the fishing pole and grab a donut, thinking over the last few days. They are all in a haze, and I don't remember much. A tug on my line distracts me for a bit, while I reel in my first fish of the day. He's a keeper, so I toss him in the cooler and recast.

As morning fades to afternoon, I grab the sandwich I packed and a beer. The beer is my dad's favorite, but I never much cared for it. This is for him. Brynn would laugh at me, I'm sure. I make a face, as I chug it down.

"Well, Dad. What a year." I start. "I gave up a job many chefs only dream of in New York City. Moved home, got a kiwi thrown at me, reconnected with Brynn, and somehow, she forgave me. How could she do that?"

I toss the empty beer can down in the cabin for me to clean up later.

"The restaurants are doing well. But somehow, I feel more at home, when I'm in the kitchen at Sunset. I hope you're okay with that. You're missed, and how it's been a year, I don't know. I forgot for a while. Forgot that you were gone, and that I was supposed to be mourning you; that I wasn't supposed to be happy. Brynn made me forget. She made me feel whole, until it all came slamming back in my face."

Then, just like my dad is pulling the strings, my phone rings. It takes me a minute to realize what it is, because we never used to get cell service out here. Pulling out my phone, I have three bars. When did that happen? It's Kade calling, so I almost don't pick up, but figure I better make sure everything is okay.

"Hey, man. What's up?" I ask.

There's a pause, before Kade speaks. "Have you been drinking?" He asks.

"Just a beer," I say.

"Sounds like more than just one." He says.

"Call to hound me on my drinking choices?" I ask.

He sighs, "No, I called to see how you are doing, and if you wanted company." He says.

"Well, I might have said yes, if you called before sunup, but I'm already out on the boat, and even caught a fish." I chuckle.

"Mmm. So, you did go?" He says.

That throws me.

"Why wouldn't I go?"

"Well, maybe because you have Brynn so upset that she hasn't been out of bed, since yesterday. She's been trying to give you space, but I think you broke her." Kade says, and I realize I said the last part out loud.

A vice squeezes my heart, and it's the first time I've felt anything in days. It comes out and hits me so hard I gasp and lean forward, gripping my chest over my heart.

"I love her with everything that I am. She's it for me. I know that, and there's no one else for me. But I finally get what she went through, and I have no idea how she forgave me, because I can't forgive me." I say the words that have been circling in my head for days.

"Why don't you ask her that, instead of punishing her for doing it?" He says with a clip in his voice.

The vice around my heart tightens even more. That's what I

have been doing, isn't it? Pushing her away, because I couldn't understand it, instead of pulling her in and thanking her every day for it.

I don't say anything to Kade, because I have no words.

"Lin is with her now. As your friend, I know what today is. But tomorrow, either get your shit together and fix this or let her go, because we both know she deserves better. Hell, if it was anyone else, and they hurt her like this, I'd be kicking their ass right now, anniversary or not." He says, and then hangs up without another word.

I toss my phone down on the chair and lay down on the bench seat, rubbing my chest. Even the mention of letting her go, is almost too much to handle. But Kade is right, I need to get my shit together and fix this one way or another. To move past this, I have to find a way to forgive myself.

I close my eyes against the blinding sun and try to come up with a game plan.

* * *

I'm surrounded by the whole town, and wearing a tux, I couldn't be happier, as I watch Brynn walk down the beach to me in the most beautiful wedding dress I've ever seen.

Her smile is blinding, and I don't think I've seen her anymore gorgeous than she is right now. My heart races, as she walks up next to me.

She reaches up and wipes the tears off my face that I didn't even know were there, before she cups my face and looks me in the eyes.

"I didn't know I could love someone so much or be loved so much.

218

Thank you for that. I love you, Jasper Adams, and I can't wait to be your wife." Brynn says.

I open my mouth to tell her how much I love her, but my dad walks up beside her first, and I feel like I swallowed my tongue.

"She's beautiful, isn't she?" He asks.

"She is. Always has been." I say.

My dad smiles at me, before reaching over to hug me.

"I always knew you'd end up here. It was going to be a bumpy road, but I knew you two were meant to be together." He nods at Brynn, who just smiles at us.

"How did you know?" I ask him.

"You always got up in your head too much. You'd forget to be thankful for what's in front of you. It doesn't matter how someone forgives you, just as long as they do. If they can forgive you, there's no reason you can't forgive yourself. I forgive you, Brynn forgives you, and your mother forgives you. What are you holding on to?" He looks at me and shakes his head.

"Relationships aren't easy. If they were, they wouldn't be worth a damn. You have to fight, Jasper. Do you hear me?" He grips both my shoulders, his smile is gone, and he looks serious.

"You have to fight. Promise me." He says, almost in a panic.

I'm not sure what is wrong, but I know I'd do anything for my dad.

"I promise," I say, as a blinding, white light takes over.

"Tell your mother I love her. And remember to fight, Jasper!" My dad says, his voice fading, as the white light takes over.

I sit up gasping, and realize it was all just a dream. One that seemed so real. Too real. A flash of white light followed by the crack of thunder jerks me to the present. A storm has rolled in, while I was sleeping. I quickly get the boat heading back towards the harbor.

The dream was so real, and I want it too bad. To marry Brynn. That's the most important thing, and she's the most important thing. What the hell have I been doing?

Another flash of lightning, and the waves start to toss the boat around. The sky opens up, and it down pours, making visibility almost nothing.

Brynn is going to kill me. What was I thinking, going out on a boat? After her parents died like this. I didn't even check the weather, I just went. It's like I wanted to do something she couldn't forgive, but I need her to know how sorry I am.

I want her to know how amazing she is. I need her to know how much I love her. I need her to know that I need *her*. The boat is being tossed around, like it weighs nothing. But I start to see some of the lights from town. If I can just get into the inlet, the water will be calmer.

I reach for the life jacket and struggle to get it on, while making sure the boat stays on course. Once it's on, I try to gather my surroundings a bit more. There's light from two other boats nearby, telling me they weren't prepared for the storm either. Both boats are bigger than mine, though.

I turn back to concentrate on getting home. I check my GPS to make sure I'm still on the right path. When I look up, I see the wave, coming right at me, and it's too late to do anything. The boat slams to the side and spins, jerking me around and lurching me forward.

I go flying, like a rag doll. I try to hold on to the wheel, but that propels me forward. My head hits the wheel. A blinding pain fills my head just before everything goes black.

Chapter 33

Brynn

I hate storms. I feel like I should tattoo that across my forehead. It's no secret, and the worst part is this area is known for storms that pop up in a matter of hours. Like this one.

I stare out over the beach and continue pacing the back porch of The Sunset Inn.

"I'm sure he's fine. Probably got to the dock and had another beer," Lin says.

The problem is her voice betrays her. She's just as worried as I am. Kade told us about his call. He could tell Jasper had a few beers. There's no way he can navigate in this storm after drinking. Most people couldn't do it sober. Add in that it's been a few years, since he's been on the water, and it's not looking good.

I finally break and pull out my phone to try his cell.

"It's going straight to voice mail," I tell them.

"He could have turned it off, after Kade called. Remember, his dad loved to fish, because there was no cell service. Though, after the storm earlier this year, they put up a stronger cell tower, so now, there's service where there wasn't before." She says.

I shake my head and call his mom.

"Hello, dear. Did Jasper make it over there, before the storm hit?" His mom asks, as calm as pie.

"What?" I ask.

"He said he was going to work the dinner shift there tonight. He should have gotten in, before this storm hit. Damn thing popped out of nowhere." She says.

"He's not here. I was calling to see if he made it home, before the storm," I tell her.

She's silent for a few minutes, and I can almost hear the gears in her head turning.

"Okay, dear. I'm going to have to call you back." She says in a very calm voice that you can tell is forced and hangs up.

I pull the phone away and just look at it. She was calm, but I can read between the lines. When I look up at Lin and Kade, I know they're thinking what I'm thinking. He isn't here, and he isn't home. He was drinking on a boat, and now, there's a storm.

"Brynn, look at me." Kade walks over to me and places his hands on my shoulder. He bends his knees to look into my eyes.

"It's nothing. I'm willing to bet he's at the dock passed out." He says.

"That's what Lin and I told each other about our parents," I say, looking over at Lin.

When I head back to my room, both Lin and Kade follow. I grab my windbreaker and keys.

"You're not going out in this!" Lin says.

"If it was Kade on the boat, what would you do right now?" I ask her.

Her eyes go stormy. "I'd go down to the docks to check myself, and then I'd check in the dockmaster to see, when he was last heard from." She says.

"Then you know what I'm doing," I tell her.

* * *

I'm not one bit surprised to find Jasper's mom in the dockmaster's office. She's going on and on to poor Allen about how they need to get someone out to look for her son.

She doesn't stop talking, when I walk in, and just opens her arms, pulling me to her side.

"Lisa, give me a minute, okay?" Allen says in a calm voice to Mrs. Adams.

She nods, before taking a deep breath.

"His boat hasn't come back." She says.

My heart sinks. In my gut, I knew this would be what I heard, but hearing it, makes it all the more real. Tears fill my eyes, as she pulls me into her, and I bury my face in her neck.

"Okay, a call went into the Coast Guard from another ship, saying a smaller fishing boat wrecked just outside the inlet. They just got there and verified it's the boat Jasper took out. He's unconscious but alive. They're airlifting him to the hospital in Jacksonville over there by Camp Lejeune. That's all I know." Allen says.

With a shaky hand, I call Lin and Kade and relay what we were just told.

"Don't move. I'll be there in ten minutes to drive you. Lin says that's a two hour drive in this weather, and neither of you is in any condition to be behind a wheel." Kade says.

"He's a good boy." Mrs. Adams says, as we sit down and wait for Kade.

The drive to the hospital feels like it takes days. I look at the clock, thinking at least ten minutes have passed, and it's barely been a minute. Kade and Lin are talking and trying to help, but neither me nor Jasper's mom is paying much attention. We're sitting in the back seat, holding each other's hand and staring out of the window.

All I can think is there's no way the world is this cruel to do this to me twice. What the hell have I done in my life to deserve this? Was I a serial killer in a past life? That's the only way to explain this.

We rush in, and Mrs. Adams gives the receptionist our info, and we're directed to the right unit, where she once again relates the information.

"Mrs. Adams, your son is currently in surgery. If you will wait here, as soon as the doctor is done, he will come out and talk to you." The nurse says.

"What is he in surgery for?" I ask.

She looks at me, and then back to Mrs. Adams.

"I'm sorry. Are you family?" She asks.

"Yes." Mrs. Adams says sternly, before I can say anything.

The nurse looks at the computer again.

"He was rushed in, so I don't have a lot of information right now. I just know he's in surgery for his leg. If I had more, I'd tell you, but I just don't have anything else." She says, looking sorry.

Then, she glances up at Lin and Kade, and her eyes go wide, and I know she recognizes Kade. The Island is used to him by now, so it's been a while, since we have had to deal with people, fangirling over him, while we are out, and I'm so not in the mood right now. Thankfully, the nurse regains her composure and offers a smile.

"Come on, let's sit down." Lin takes my hand.

I just shake my head and start pacing the waiting room. It's set up in a way that I can walk in a circle around the twenty something chairs in here. Jasper's mom has the same idea.

Kade leans over and whispers something in Lin's ear, and she nods, before Kade goes and talks to the nurse. They discuss something, before another nurse joins with a tablet. Once he walks back over, I look at him and he shrugs.

"I thought it would be better to get him a private room, since I'm guessing neither of you is leaving his side, and you'll need someplace to rest, too." He says.

This man is amazing, and the best person I could have asked for, for Lin. He's like a brother to me. I don't think, as I go over to him and hug him tightly, and he hugs me back just as tight.

"Well, if a room gets me a hug, please don't kiss me, when I bring you food." He jokes.

I give a dry chuckle. "Thank you," I say.

Jasper's mom hugs him as well, but it's interrupted by a doctor.

"Family of Jasper Adams?" He says.

"Here." All four of us say. He nods and walks over.

"Jasper came in unconscious and still is. He hit his head pretty hard, so that isn't uncommon. We did an MRI, and everything looks good. He's very lucky. There's no internal bleeding, but his leg had a nasty gash on it, and the bone splintered. I normally wouldn't have done surgery, but because of how deep the cut was, I wanted to make sure to get it cleaned

225

and go ahead and set the bone now. Then, we can get him recovering as fast as possible. Be prepared, when you see him, he was banged up pretty bad." The doctor says.

He goes into some detail on what he did to Jasper's leg, but all I can think about is that he's alive.

Mrs. Adams sags into the closest chair, and I fall into Kade's side.

"Right now, it's a wait and see if he'll wake up. If he wakes up, I feel he will make a full recovery. As soon as he's settled in his room, a nurse will be in to get you. It shouldn't be more than about twenty minutes." He says.

Mrs. Adams and I both nod, and Kade thanks the doctor and shakes his hand, before we all sit down.

"If he wakes up." I murmur.

"Don't think like that," Lin says, but I'm not sure how else to think.

It seems like hours, before the nurse comes out to direct us back to see Jasper.

"You're all family?" She asks, as she eyes Kade. It's obvious she recognizes him.

He pulls Lin to his side and kisses the top of her head, but it's Jasper's mom who speaks up.

"Yes, we are for the fifth time in the last hour. Now, if you will take us to see my son, that would be great." She snaps.

The nurse's eyes go wide, and this is when Kade turns on the charm.

"She's worried about her son. But yes, we're all family, so if you could, just show us back." He says.

"But you're Kade Markson." She says, like she's going to argue the fact that there's no way he's related to Jasper.

"Jasper is my brother-in-law. Lin and I got married recently."

226

When he smiles down at Lin, he misses the sad look on the nurse's face, but she nods and leads us down a maze of corridors.

When we get to the end of a hall, we find him in a private room. With the exception of the hospital bed, it looks like it could be a hotel suite. Tile floors with a room for the bed and equipment. There's a sliding frosted glass door that closes the bed area off from the sitting area that has a couch and love seat, a few chairs, a coffee table, and a TV.

Jasper's mom and I see him at the same time and rush to his side. She on one side of the bed, and me on the other.

"Can we hold his hand?" I ask the nurse.

"Yes, just be careful of any bruises. His leg with the cast shouldn't be jostled, but his hands are fine." She says. She also points out the call buttons, if we need anything and heads out.

Kade brings over a chair from the sitting area for both Jasper's mom and me, as Lin comes in, holding a pamphlet.

"So, those chairs each recline back into a makeshift bed, but the love seat and sofa both have pull out beds. I've never seen anything like this." She looks around the room. "There's a fully equipped bathroom, so you two have no reason to leave. We'll bring you food and anything else you need."

"Thank you." I croak out, but it doesn't look like Jasper's mom heard us, until she speaks.

"That's perfect, because I'm not leaving his side." She says.

"Neither am I," I say.

Our eyes meet, and she gives me a quick nod. We both may be mad as hell at him, but we will fight to make sure he lives, so we have the opportunity to yell at him.

It's nice to be on the same side.

* * *

I jerk awake to find I'm still in the hospital room. I had fallen asleep in the chair with my head, leaning on the bed right next to Jasper's hand. My hand is still in his, as I have yet to let go of it.

Across from me, his mom sits, and she gives me a forced smile.

"Have you slept at all?" I ask her.

"I dozed off a bit, but I think I'm going to go for a walk, get some coffee, and find some food. I want to call and check in on the restaurants, too." She says.

My eyes shoot to Lin.

"We already checked in; everything is fine. The town knows what happened, and they're helping. Rich has The Sunset under control, and he's helping watch Sunrise. Nate has been stopping in every few hours to check on things, and he's also been by both your restaurants, Mrs. Adams. The kitchen is under control. Everyone is stepping up." Lin says.

"Okay." I nod, as Jasper's mom stands up and leans over to place a kiss on Jasper's forehead.

"I'll be here," I tell her. I have no plans of leaving this room, but they don't need to worry about that right now.

Mrs. Adams walks out of the door, and I turn to Lin and Kade.

"I'd like a few minutes alone with him. Maybe, you guys can go find us some food?" I ask.

Kade nods. "Burgers sound good? I noticed a burger place down the road."

Lin comes over and hugs me.

"Yes, a burger sounds great," I say.

Kade takes Lin's hand, and they leave to grab food.

When I'm finally alone, I turn to Jasper. His leg is propped up on a pillow and in a temporary cast from surgery. He has bruises everywhere on his arms, a big one on his forehead, where he hit his head, a black eye, and a few scrapes on his face.

Tears flood my eyes again. Mostly, because I hate seeing him like this, and part of it is also from anger. I try to latch on to the anger.

"I'm so mad at you. Instead of talking to me and pulling me in to help you, you pushed me away. You acted like I had no idea how it feels. Guess what? I do know what it feels like. Every year, it's still hard to breathe, when I think of that day. More than that, I'm even madder at you for taking the boat out, after you knew how I felt about it. How dare you put me through this again?"

Stopping, I wipe the tears, falling down my face.

"Do you have any idea how scared I was, when the storm came in? I tried to reason it away, like I did with my parents that you just went home. But when I called your mom, you weren't there." I choke up.

"I can't lose you too, Jasper. Not again. It would break me in a way I can't come back from. I need you to fight. Fight, so I can properly be mad at you, when you wake up. But most of all fight because I love you." I say and squeeze his hand.

I lay my head on the side of the bed and cry.

"I want to hear those words every day, Firefly." His grainy voice fills the air.

I have to be imagining it, right? But when I look up, he's staring right at me.

Chapter 34

Jasper

Fuck, these lights are bright as hell. They make my head hurt worse than it already does.

"Lights." I croak. And a minute later, the lights dim, and the rattle of metal signals the curtains over the window have been closed.

I crack my eyes open again, and Brynn is standing next to the bed.

"Water," I say and take a few sips, once she brings the straw to my lips.

"I need to get the nurse." She says, putting the water down.

I reach for her hand, which makes every muscle I never knew I had hurt.

"Say it again," I ask her. I need to make sure I wasn't dreaming, because the last thing I remember, is fighting the storm in the boat, and now, I'm here and everything hurts.

Her eyes soften, and her face flushes with emotion. Her eyes glisten, like she's on the verge of crying.

"I love you, Jasper." She says, barely above a whisper.

I close my eyes and sigh. The words heal me in a way nothing in this hospital can. I open my eyes to find Brynn watching me.

"I'm calling the nurse." She says, walking around the bed to push a button.

A moment later a nurse comes in.

"He's awake. Keep the light low, because they're bothering him." Brynn says, after there's a knock on the door and another nurse walks in.

After that, it's a flurry of activity, as a few doctors and nurses come in to talk to me and check me out. Brynn's hand never leaves mine, and I couldn't tell you what any of them said.

My head is swimming. They asked so many questions, and all spew so much medical jargon that I just wanted them to stop. Kade and Lin came in with food for Brynn and have been trying to get her to eat. When my mom walked in, she pushed a doctor out of the way to get to my side.

"As soon as you get out of here, you're in big trouble, do you hear me? I have enough to worry about without you trying to put me in the grave with your father. Stupid boy." She mumbles, as the doctor keeps talking.

When the nurses and doctors leave, I turn to Brynn. I'm tired, and whatever medicine they gave me, is making me sleepy as hell.

"What happened?" I ask.

Brynn seems to know what I mean. She always does.

"The boat that called in your accident says a wave came and knocked yours on the side. The guys who pulled you from the boat said you were unconscious, hit your head on the steering wheel, and then got tossed around a bit. At least, you were wearing a life vest, because it saved your life. When you didn't come back, I called your mom, and when she said you weren't

231

there, we both knew. We both went to the dockmaster who told us they were airlifting you here. Kade and Lin drove us." Brynn says.

My mom takes over, "You were in surgery, when we got here. The doctors kept saying you were very lucky, but they had to go in, clean your leg, get the bleeding stopped, set it, and sew you back up. You will be in a cast for a while. Serves you right." Mom gives me the stink eye.

I know this version of my mom. She was so scared, and now that I'm fine, she's relieved and pissed at me for scaring her. Hell, I'm pissed at myself for scaring her, too.

"When you're released, you won't be able to be in the kitchen, until the cast comes off, and that includes my kitchen. You will let me take care of you," Mom says.

"Ahhh well, that depends," I say.

"On *what?*" She asks.

I turn to look at Brynn. "On this girl. I'm sorry these meds are killing me. I promise, we will talk, but I need to close my eyes for a bit, and you need to eat." I say.

"I'll make sure she eats. Get some rest." Kade says, and I close my eyes.

* * *

When I wake up again, the room is still dark, and everything is quiet. My mom is asleep in the chair to my left, and Brynn is watching TV in the chair to my right with her hand still in mine. I give her hand a squeeze, and her eyes shoot over to mine.

"Hey." She whispers and smiles at me. "You need some more pain meds?" She asks.

"In a few. I wanted to say how sorry I am." I say, and her eyes go dark.

"Not right now, Jasper. Let's work on getting you out of here." She says.

"No, I need to say this, and you need to hear it. I was in a dark place, because when it hit me how close to the one year anniversary we were, I realized I knew how you felt all those years ago. Then, I started to wonder how you could forgive me, when I couldn't even forgive myself for not being there for you." I say, nodding towards the water.

As she brings the straw to my lips, she sighs. "It's been five years. Was I angry at you, yes, but I let all that go for me. I had to, because letting it beat me up, wasn't an option, when I had The Inn and everyone there, depending on me. When I saw you at the Farmer's Market, I had already forgiven you. That didn't mean I was ready to trust you with my heart again, or let you off the hook so easy." She says, as she sets the cup back down.

"I was trying to connect with my dad and figure out how to move forward, so that's why I got on the boat," I say, watching her purse her lips.

"I'm sorry, but it was what I needed. I realized I didn't want another day without you in my life." I tell her.

"But you don't get it! You did the one thing that would scare me the most by getting on the boat. I almost lost you the same way I lost them. It wasn't you who would have to live with it. It would have been me, losing a third person the same way, and then having to live without you." She says with tears in her eyes.

"I know, and if you can forgive me yet again, I swear I will never step foot on another boat. My days will be spent showing you how much I love you, and so you never have to spend a day without me, I promise to let you go first." I say.

She takes in a large, slow breath and bites her bottom lip.

"I love you, Brynn, and I want to marry you. Sooner rather than later, but I will wait as long as it takes for you to be ready." I say, laying my cards on the table.

She deserves so much more than a proposal from a hospital bed that I can't even get out of. Hell, I don't even have a ring, but I need her to know I'm serious about this and all in.

"Jasper…" She gasps.

"Say yes, and I will make sure to give you the proposal and wedding of your dreams. We can move into your parents' house and run The Sunset together, like we always dreamed of. I swear, every dream we talked about all those late nights, I'll make them come true. The dog, the kids, and the large family trips. All of it."

Tears are flowing down Brynn's cheeks, and all I want to do is reach over and wipe them away, but I can barely move.

"Yes." She whispers and more tears flow.

"Yes?" I smile so big that my whole face hurts, but I don't care.

"Yes!" She says more certain this time, drawing the attention of Lin, Kade, and my mom, but I don't care.

"Come here, Firefly," I say, and when her lips land on mine, I know there isn't a moment better than this.

* * *

"Do I need to move the couch? Can you get around the coffee table? Maybe, I should put the coffee table in storage for right now. No, you'll need it to put your leg up on." Brynn fires off question after question without giving me time to respond. I got out of the hospital today and decided to take the next step and move in with Brynn. I hated to do it to my mom right after the accident, but her smile, when I told her, could have lit up a Christmas tree brighter than Christmas morning. She then reminded me, daughter-in-law before grandbabies.

"It's fine where it is, I swear, and if it's not, I promise to tell you," I say, sitting on the couch and setting my crutches down.

"How are you feeling? You still have time before your next round of medicine. Are you hungry?" She says, starting down the road of never-ending questions again.

Smiling, I grab hold of her hand and pull her onto my lap.

"Don't do that. You could hurt yourself." She says.

"I'm not as fragile as you think," I say and lean in to kiss her. My fiancé.

I run my thumb over the ring on her hand, as I pull back from the kiss.

When we told Lin and Kade we were going to get married, Lin made Kade drive her all the way back here, and then back to the hospital to give me Brynn's mom's ring. She has been wearing it ever since.

My mom was over the moon to hear we are engaged and spent the rest of my hospital time, wedding planning with Brynn. Though, Brynn insisted I be out of the cast and walking on my own again for our wedding, so it will be after the season, but before Christmas. Anything she plans will be perfect.

"Tomorrow, I want to go check on the kitchen here. I need to apologize to the guys." I tell her.

"Jasper, you can't work!" She says.

Leaning in to give her another kiss.

"You can come with me. I have no plans to work. I just want to apologize and make sure they're okay. I want to run the kitchen here with you, and to do that, I need to make things right with them." I say.

"Okay, but I'm going with you." She says.

"I also need to peek in at Samuel's and The Hummingbird Bar. My dad set them up to run on their own, and they do, but I wasn't very nice there either. I need to make amends and check to see if they're okay, too. If not tomorrow, then the next day. Then, I promise not to leave this room for a week." I say and start kissing her neck.

"Jasper." She moans. "We can't."

"I can't, but you can," I say and start running my hand up her thigh.

"Make you a deal. If you take a nap, we can go to the kitchen, have dinner in bed, and then we have some fun. But only if you nap, it was a long car ride." She says.

"Deal," I say.

I think I'm going to like a life time of using orgasms, as bargaining chips, because not giving them to her, isn't an option ever again.

Epilogue 1

Brynn
4 months later

"Two weddings in one year, and to think, this time last year we were making plans in case we never got married." Lin says with little hearts in her eyes.

"I'm just glad we're getting married, before you start to show," I say and rub her belly.

Today, I get to marry Jasper. It's been hell waiting, until after the season, but he had to get his cast off and do some physical therapy. Other than the scar, he's as good as new.

Kade and Lin recently told me and Jasper they're expecting. She's only ten weeks along, and they haven't made it public yet, but I'm so thrilled to have a little niece or nephew on the way.

"Okay, let's get this tiara on and get the full effect," Lin says, as she puts on the tiara I opted for, instead of a veil, since we're getting married on the beach.

The door to my room opens and closes, and Jasper's mom walks in.

"Alright, I have booze. Need some liquid courage to walk

down the aisle? Because I'm dragging you one way or the other." She says, and we laugh.

"No cold feet. I'm ready." I tell her.

I asked her to walk me down the aisle, because she's going to be family. She took care of me, when my parents died. Even though, Jasper and I weren't together, and she has always been my biggest cheerleader.

"Good, now I have a gift for you." She says. "Something old. This was my mother's, and she passed it to me on her wedding day. I never had a girl, but you are like a daughter to me, so I'm passing it to you on your wedding day." Mrs. Adams holds up this beautiful antique hair comb.

"Oh my, gosh!" I gasp.

It's silver with diamonds in a swirl pattern with pearls mixed in. She comes around and fixes it into my hair.

"Now, Jasper took care of the something new." She hands me a large square box with a bow wrapped around it. There's a card tucked into the bow, so I read that first.

Brynn,

I remember the first day I saw you. You had on that bright, pink shirt you wore all the time, until you outgrew it. The one with a glittery pineapple on it. You also had on white shorts and sandals. Your hair was in those pigtail French braids you loved to wear.

I knew at the age of seven I wanted to be near you. I needed to be your friend, and I didn't understand the pull, then.

On our first date, you wore that blue spaghetti strapped, long Bohemian, beach dress. There was just enough of a dip that I had to fight all night not to stare at your tits. After that, you in that dress showed up in many of my late night fantasies.

The night we lost our virginity together, we had spent the day at the beach. You were wearing a black one piece that had the cutouts over your stomach. You wore a multi-colored striped cover-up dress over it.

When I opened my eyes in that hospital room, you were wearing shorts and one of my Hummingbird Bar shirts.

Every important memory of you is seared into my brain, and today, is another one. I can't wait to see you in your wedding dress; memorize how it hugs your body and shows off your curves.

Then tonight, I will memorize what it looks like, as I peel it off of you, as I make love to my wife.

I love you, Firefly. This necklace is one of the first of many ways I plan to spoil you. Please, wear it today. Mom assures me it goes with your dress.

Your husband,
Jasper

I gasp, when I open it. The necklace has diamonds in a flower swirl with pearls mixed in just like the comb his mom gave me. Lin helps me put it on, and he's right, it looks great with my dress.

My dress is a long, flowy tulle, and the bodice has these embedded lace flowers, and when the sunlight hits them, they almost glitter. It's just a bit much for a beach wedding, but when I saw it, I knew I had to have it.

Lin steps up to me next.

"I've got your something borrowed and something blue. I want these back, because they were a gift from Kade." She says and holds up the most beautiful diamond and Sapphire teardrop earrings.

"Oh, these are beautiful," I tell her and put them on.

"We also wrapped some blue ribbon in your bouquet just to

be safe." Lin smiles.

I turn to take in my complete ensemble in the mirror, as Lin stands beside me in her lavender bridesmaid dress. It's a floor length chiffon that flows like mine. It's an A-line with spaghetti straps, and the sales lady said it was a silhouette style. I just know that it's flowy enough to hide any baby bump, and it somehow matches mine. Lin looks stunning in it.

I turn to face her. "We did it, you know," I say with a smile.

"Did what?" She asks.

"We're getting our happily ever after. You're already growing our family. We'll raise them like our parents raised us. To be best friends and grow up next door together and running The Inns together." I say.

The smile that takes over Lin's face is huge.

"Let's get you married." She says.

* * *

Jasper

The town spared no details for this wedding. It's at sunset on the beach in front of Sunset Inn. There are lanterns with candles lining the rose petal covered aisle. Behind me is a beautiful arch that will frame us with tulle and fairy lights, during the ceremony.

There are five empty seats up front with candles in them. Two for Brynn's parents, two for Lin's parents, and one for my dad.

Before I can start down the emotional ride of not having my dad here, the ceremony starts. But when Brynn steps off the porch and makes her way to me, nothing else matters.

Her dress reflects off the candlelight, as she walks down the aisle. She's smiling from ear to ear, and I memorize every detail about this moment. Her dress, and the way her hair is pulled up in curls. The tiara, and the necklace I gave her. It all works perfectly together.

When she is finally in front of me, I feel like I can breathe again, and I can't stop smiling. I nod and say all the right words, though what they are, I can't tell you, so I'm thankful my mom assigned someone to video the whole ceremony.

When I slide the ring onto Brynn's finger, the symbol that she's mine, and she carries my mark on her, is such a turn on I have to think about something else, so I don't pop wood in front of the whole town.

Brynn sliding the ring onto my finger has the same effect on me, and thankfully, it's time to kiss the bride. A slow, possessive kiss that shows her and everyone around us what she means to me.

"I'm proud to introduce for the first time, Mr. and Mrs. Jasper Adams." Josh says. Josh has presided over many weddings here on the beach, so it only seemed natural he'd marry us as well.

After we walk down the aisle and back into The Sunset Inn, I pull Brynn to our room. Construction started on her parents' place two weeks ago, updating the kitchen and bathrooms and repainting. As soon as it's ready, we're moving in, and until then, we're staying here in Brynn's room.

I pin my bride to the door, when we're in the room and kiss her like I wanted to on the beach, only I don't want anyone else to see her like this. I run my hands all over her body, and as beautiful as the dress is, I'm hating how it's keeping me from her body right now.

"My wife, I want you so much. Think we can skip the reception?" I ask, knowing we can't, nor would I let her, because I want her to have this memory.

She groans, before answering me. "We have to go out there but just think. All the teasing will lead to an explosive night." She says.

"And the worst case of blue balls I have ever had." I groan, already in pain of wanting her so much.

She chuckles, "Do you really want to tell our kids the reason there are no reception photos is because Daddy couldn't stay out of Mommy long enough."

"Maybe, when they're eighteen, sure." I sigh, but I know she's right. "Okay, let's go show you off, but be prepared to not wear clothes for the next few days."

"Deal."

* * *

Brynn

Married life is amazing, but Lin was right, changing my name on everything has been a huge pain in the ass. Jasper went with me to help as much as he could, but even he was shocked at how much there was to do.

Construction on the villas is chugging along, and we're set

to open this spring and already have a waiting list of people who want that first booking, as soon as they're ready. I think that's more thanks to Kade's name than anything.

Today, Jasper and I are cuddled on Lin and Kade's couch, watching the reality TV show my chef ditched me for that kicked all this off. As pissed as I was at him, I do owe him for pushing Jasper and me together.

The show is on week two, and George made it past the first elimination, and the guy they let go of was horrible, so we agreed with that decision.

Today, as we watch, George sets part of his food on fire and almost falls, running around the kitchen, getting what he needs, and I take small joy in that. Petty, I know.

I'm pretty sure he's going to make it to the next round, until it's his turn in front of the judges. They don't have anything good to say about his food, but then, one judge chimes in.

"We heard that you left your last job high and dry to come on this show. That you didn't even give them time to get a replacement, after a big storm hit the area. Is that true?" The judge asks.

"Oh my, God. Who told them?" I ask.

"Kade, it was you, wasn't it?" Lin smacks his arm.

"Well, I wasn't taking any chances. I made the call, before everything worked out with Jasper." He says with a smile.

After a few more remarks, George is cut from the show on round two, and we all cheer.

"I wonder what he's doing now for work," I say more to myself than anything.

"I wondered too, so I used some contacts and found out he's a line chef at a Las Vegas buffet and not a classy one either," Jasper says, and we all laugh.

243

Yep, life is working out just like it should.

Epilogue 2

Jasper
5 Years Later

Just like Brynn's parents used to do, we're taking July 4th off and spending it with our kids. Kade and Lin are over at our house, along with my mom and Kade's parents. My mom has taken on the grandmother role to both our kids, and Kade and Lin's, too.

"Think this is going to backfire on us?" Kade says, as he nods towards where Lin and Brynn are teaching our kids how to use water guns, while we man the grill.

"Oh, it will. I bet by tomorrow they'll have even tried to fire them off in the house." I laugh, and Kade groans.

"Your mom knew what she was doing buying those for them." He says.

"Oh yes, she did." I smile.

Brynn looks up at me from across the yard and smiles. Life couldn't be any better than this.

The girls got the large family they wanted, and if the fact that Lin is skipping the margaritas my mom is making is any hint, it's about to be expanding, too.

We may be the only locals not out on the water today, but after my hospital stay, Kade and I both made a promise to the girls, no more boats. After that scare, it wasn't a hardship to give them that. I'm perfectly content to fish off the new fishing pier the town put in. The lighthouse is being reconstructed on the old one, so they have stopped people from fishing there.

After we eat, my mom comes up to me. "Kade's parents and I are taking the kids down for the Main Street parade to give Mom and Dad some alone time." She winks at me.

It's become a tradition after lunch, the parade is grandparents only. As soon as they leave with the kid's, Lin smiles at Brynn.

"See you in a few hours." She says over her shoulder, and Kade hauls her next door to their house, and I pull Brynn inside.

"I think this is my favorite part of July 4th," I mumble, as my lips crash into hers.

"Couch." She says around my kiss.

We got a new couch last month, and ever since, she has been hinting at wanting to break it in today.

"Clothes off, and then get on the couch on your knees facing the back," I say, and she hurries to obey my command.

Watching her every move, as I undress, is one of my favorite things. I love Brynn's body even more after she has given me two amazing kids.

Once she's in position with her back to me, I walk up behind her and rub my hands up her back and back down to her hips.

"I saw the look you were giving me, Firefly. With Lin being pregnant, you want to catch up. You were giving me the please put a baby inside of me eyes. You know what those eyes do to me." I say, as I line my cock up at her entrance.

246

"Please…" She starts to beg, and I thrust hard into her.

She throws one hand up against the wall behind the couch and screams my name. With the kids gone, we don't have to be quiet.

My hands grip her hips, as I continue to thrust in and out of her hard and fast, not giving her time to adjust. She arches and throws her head back. Her long, brown hair flows down, and I grab a fist full of it and wrap it around my hand.

I use her hair to turn her head to the side. "I love you, Firefly." I grit out.

"I love you too, my husband." She says, and I have to grind my teeth, so I don't cum then and there.

She has found that hearing her call me her husband is the biggest turn on for me. Even after all these years, I love hearing it.

I lean over her and nip at her ear. The change in angle is all she needs.

"Oh, God. Don't stop, don't stop. Don't you dare stop!" She screams.

"Wouldn't dream of it, Firefly," I say and thrust a bit harder, pushing her over the edge.

Her pussy clamps down on my cock, and I barely get another thrust in, before I'm cumming right along with her.

I wrap myself around her waist to stop her from collapsing, as I fall onto the couch, taking her with me.

"Give me a minute, and then we can go clean up and do that again in the shower." She says.

God, I love my wife.

* * *

As the storm rolls in an hour after fireworks wrap up, and the kids are in bed, we sit on the back porch and watch it come in. I understand her aversion to them even more, but we like to sit on the porch in each other's arms together.

"Did Mom tell you the mayor asked about turning the old hotel above Samuel's back into a hotel?" I ask Brynn.

"No." She says.

Daniel ran for mayor last year and won hands down. He's done some inventive things to restore the town's history, like rebuilding the lighthouse.

"Yeah, he found a bunch of history on it and approached Mom the other day. She asked about having guests above a seafood restaurant, and he doesn't seem worried. She and I are going over the plans. I guess, he wants control over the renovations to bring it back as close to what it was back then with modern plumbing and all. Mom isn't sure she wants the headache of running it." I tell her.

"Sunset on Main." Brynn laughs.

"Too bad it faces east." I smile and kiss her head.

"We should talk to Kade and Lin. I bet they'd be happy to help out." She says.

"I think so, too." I agree.

Kade has taken to running The Inn and the villas, like he was born to do it. Watching him and Lin together, you'd never know he was a famous movie star, before his time here on The Island.

As for Brynn and me, we got our dream. I run the kitchen at The Sunset Inn, and she runs The Inn. I have a great team set up at both my dad's restaurants in town and stop in once a week to check on them. For the most part, the chefs there have it under control.

I wouldn't give up working with my wife for anything.

When she starts shifting in her seat, I smile, thinking of what we did on the couch earlier today, and then again in the shower.

"Sore, Firefly?" I ask her.

"A little bit, but it's the good kind of sore."

"Let's go upstairs, so I can make you feel better." I stand and take her hand.

Just when I think life can't get any better, the girl of my dreams goes to sleep in my arms every night.

I thank the stars above for second chances.

* * *

Make sure you read Lin and Kade story in **Sunrise: Chasing the Sun Duet #1**!

Want another small town book to get away with? Don't miss **Take Me To The River**. A perfect mountain getaway book.

Want more second chance romances? Don't miss **The Cowboy and His Best Friend** and also don't miss **Texting Titan**!

* * *

Get free books!
Join Kaci Rose's romance-only newsletter to get free books, subscriber only deals, and stay up to date with the newest releases.

Join Kaci Rose's Newsletter.
https://www.kacirose.com/KaciRoseBoB

* * *

Connect with Kaci Rose
Website
Facebook
Kaci Rose Reader's Facebook Group
Instagram
Twitter
Goodreads
Book Bub
Amazon
Join Kaci Rose's VIP List (Newsletter)

Other Books By Kaci Rose

See all of Kaci Rose's Books

Oakside Military Heroes Series
Saving Noah – Lexi and Noah
Saving Easton – Easton and Paisley
Saving Teddy – Teddy and Mia
Saving Levi - Levi and Mandy

Chasing the Sun Duet
Sunrise
Sunset

Rock Springs Texas Series
The Cowboy and His Runaway – Blaze and Riley
The Cowboy and His Best Friend – Sage and Colt
The Cowboy and His Obsession – Megan and Hunter
The Cowboy and His Sweetheart – Jason and Ella
The Cowboy and His Secret – Mac and Sarah
Rock Springs Weddings Novella
Rock Springs Box Set 1-5 + Bonus Content
The Cowboy and His Mistletoe Kiss – Lilly and Mike

SUNSET

The Cowboy and His Valentine – Maggie and Nick
The Cowboy and His Vegas Wedding – Royce and Anna
The Cowboy and His Angel – Abby and Greg
The Cowboy and His Christmas Rockstar – Savannah and Ford
The Cowboy and His Billionaire – Brice and Kayla

Mountain Men Of Whiskey River
Take Me To The River

Standalone Books
Stay With Me Now
Texting Titan
Accidental Sugar Daddy
She's Still The One

Please Leave a Review!

I love to hear from my readers! Please leave a review of what you thought of this book!

Made in the USA
Columbia, SC
30 January 2024